# Martyred

The Story of Saint Lorenzo Ruiz

# Martyred

## The Story of Saint Lorenzo Ruiz

By Susan Tan

Pauline

BOOKS & MEDIA

Boston

Library of Congress Cataloging-in-Publication Data

Tan, Susan, 1960-
  [Martyrdom of St. Lorenzo Ruiz]
  Martyred : the story of Saint Lorenzo Ruiz / by Susan Tan. -- First North American edition.
    pages cm
  Originally published as The martyrdom of St. Lorenzo Ruiz. Pasay City, Philippines : Paulines Pub. House, 2007.
  ISBN-13: 978-0-8198-4934-2
  ISBN-10: 0-8198-4934-0
  1. Ruiz, Lorenzo, -1637--Fiction. 2. Christian saints--Philippines--History--17th century--Fiction. 3. Martyrdom--Christianity--History--17th century--Fiction. 4. Japan--Civilization--1600-1868--Fiction. I. Title.
  PS3620.A68365M37 2014
  813'.6--dc23
                    2013026334

The Scripture quotations contained herein are from the *New Revised Standard Version Bible: Catholic Edition,* copyright © 1989, 1993, Division of Christian Education of the National Council of the Churches of Christ in the United States of America. Used by permission. All rights reserved.

Cover design by Mary Joseph Peterson, FSP

Cover art by Jeff Falerni

Originally published by Daughters of St. Paul Philippines in English as *The Martyrdom of St. Lorenzo Ruiz: The Last Witness Among Them* by Susan Tan

Copyright © 2007 Susan Tan and Daughters of St. Paul Philippines
2650 F.B. Harrison St., 1300 Pasay City, Philippines

This is a novelized retelling of the life of Saint Lorenzo Ruiz and his companions. While the main characters are real and the account of their martyrdom is historical, elements of this story—including characters, conversations, and events—are fictional products of the author's imagination.

First North American edition, 2014

Published by Pauline Books & Media, 50 Saint Pauls Avenue, Boston, MA 02130-3491

Printed in the U.S.A.

www.pauline.org

Pauline Books & Media is the publishing house of the Daughters of St. Paul, an international congregation of women religious serving the Church with the communications media.

1 2 3 4 5 6 7 8 9                     18 17 16 15 14

*Do not invite death by the error of your life, or bring destruction by the works of your hands; because God did not make death, and he does not delight in the death of the living.*

—Wisdom 1:12–13

*The last enemy to be destroyed is death.*

—1 Corinthians 15:26

# Prologue

Autumn arrived with an annual visitor to Nagasaki, a remote seaport hemmed in by steep mountains on the island of Kyushu in southwest Japan. Jomei stood, not as physically tall as he once was, but with great presence nonetheless. He very much anticipated his guest's arrival, though he was uncertain how long he could sustain this annual reunion. It was true that Jomei had been a samurai, but he was not as agile as the spirit that came to meet him in his old age. Yet Jomei anticipated this guest with increasing devotion, as one looks forward to a good friend's arrival from afar. Opening the door, his white hair caught the breeze as he bowed. "Lorenzo," he whispered.

Jomei's guest was, in truth, a ghost from long ago—outside of time and ageless. He was not unlike the spirits Jomei's ancestors had called to in their need. But this was no divinity or demigod, nor did he come with vengeance to punish Jomei. The spirit's presence was strangely one of comfort, even solace. Yet, friendship could never have grown between them when the man was alive. The doors to outsiders had long since slammed shut with the shogun's rigid policy of isolating Japan. And a tormentor and his victim are unlikely companions. *There are things a man must live with and bear as a mark upon his soul.*

At one time Jomei might have put an end to his existence in *seppuku*,[1] death by a self-inflicted mortal wound with his own sword. It was a horrible but quick escape from life and its burdens. But such an end troubled him. *If this life is all there is—how could it be justified?* Still more the persistence of something he could not understand pursued him like an overpowering wave at sea as it plunges down on its poor victims. Jomei had lived honorably, beyond what any standard might have demanded of him. Yet there was a greatness he could not fully comprehend. He had glimpsed a freedom and height he could not successfully scale, a depth he could not wholly explore apart from the powerful force of his will to live. The hope of reaching it had cost Jomei something more than honor.

He carried in remarkable detail the memory of what had initially caused him shame. Yet gauging from the annual visits which came at the anniversary of his guest's execution, death seemed to be rendered harmless because it was without lasting victory. *Is death no more than a momentary sting? Perhaps for some.*

The circumstances of their meeting were too absurd to nurture any bond of brotherhood between them. Instead, Jomei and his visitor were bound by torture and rage. For a time they had shared a spot on the earth and their destinies were forever linked because of it. Throughout the 590 mile journey from Okinawa to Nagasaki, each of them made small decisions. But it was not as if either of them had a real choice in the matter. The outcome was predetermined, but how it played out was the result of a conscious decision to believe or not to believe, to die victorious or in defeat. Between Jomei and his guest, it was a matter of faith.

Lorenzo Ruiz had died in the execution of six men, all of them Catholics. They were led up a hill overlooking Nagasaki Bay and thrown into a well. Hung from their feet, their heads dangled above sharpened stakes, while their rotting flesh was invaded by feasting maggots. They perished through hemorrhage and asphyxiation. Lorenzo Ruiz was not the last to die. Still, it was Ruiz who made the most lasting impression in Jomei's mind because he was neither a cleric nor Japanese. He had died on a Wednesday thirty years before—September 29, 1637—three days after Jomei had ordered his men to slice gashes into their heads.

Jomei fulfilled the duty his position demanded of him. He had planned and ordered their torture and execution. Jomei could still see the iron stain and smell the metallic odor of blood in the execution pits. He could hear their groans rising amid the dampened walls. Their crime was absolutely clear. They were foreigners; and worse, Christians. But peace was something that had eluded him ever since.

And yet on the anniversary of his execution, the unseen guest arrived and lodged with Jomei in his home. The encounters were cordial and informal, like the reunion of two comrades swapping stories of past battles. They were also brief, all but concluding as soon as they commenced. Jomei was always left with the misery of wanting more. This only worsened the heavy burdens he carried in his mind and, more grievously, in his heart.

Jomei kept a list of their names. Believing he had committed an irreversible error, he made a daily ritual of reciting them for the thirty years that had passed. Among those he had killed, Lorenzo Ruiz was the only one who was married and the head of a family. Perhaps this was what troubled Jomei most. The others were European missionaries, Dominicans, traveling with a Japanese Christian convert and a priest.

Lorenzo had been given an opportunity to renounce his faith and return home to the Philippines. He refused. The courage he summoned seemed to make him indestructible. Jomei was as intrigued as he was perplexed. *What kind of Lord did these Christians serve? How does dying in disgrace bear witness to a Master's goodness? Why would anyone sing while he languished? Insanity.*

Jomei had, on several occasions, come to the conclusion that he would have to take his own life. *This is the accepted way of the warrior.* But as he planned to redeem nothing more than personal honor, Jomei could not fight off the idea that *seppuku* presented a kind of honor that was fleeting at best, gone before it had even come into full bloom. In contrast, Ruiz's martyrdom seemed to bear a kind of infinity within it, a mystical sacrifice that extended well beyond death.

*Still, death is death is death. There is no beautiful way to die.* Truly Ruiz and his companions were made to suffer until the last drops of their blood could be shed. Yet somehow it seemed to Jomei that the blood of a martyr, though red as a warrior's, was tinged by the color of sanctity. *Why?* It was said that the martyrs had offered their lives as a sacrifice for their executioners, for the salvation of their souls. *What kind of man loves his killers?*

It was proper that their remains be thrown out to the sea after they were cremated, Jomei thought. No foreigner must find a resting place in a land that the Japanese held sacred. And yet their lifeblood had soaked the earth beneath his feet, and made it fertile for the growth of something Jomei could not have foreseen.

"Not so soon, *otouto-san,* my young brother," the old man Jomei said. He motioned with his right hand for his guest to sit across from him. "Stay a moment longer."

Jomei had prepared his household for this foreign guest, though he never breathed the visitor's name to anyone, not even to those closest to him. Content with his company, Jomei took in with relish the sight of the nearly harvested field. The work was almost finished. He and his spirit friend stayed like this for a good length of time, comfortable in each other's presence. Any added exchange of conversation would have been proof to the contrary.

"Do you hear the kettle simmering?" he asked. Jomei would not have called attention to something so mundane had his visitor been Japanese. Before tea was served it was customary to wait for the quiet sound of water beginning to boil. "My granddaughter prepares us our tea."

Aiko was growing into a fine child. Slender, with wisps of fine blue-black hair framing her face, she was no more than eleven years old. Aiko usually stayed at home with her grandfather, who taught her calligraphy and reading when she was not occupied by chores. Until a year ago, when her grandmother Chiyo was still alive, lessons in the art of serving tea had taken up most of her afternoons.

The precision and elegance of such learning betrayed the plainness of their everyday existence. Aiko's parents farmed the land they now possessed. Jomei had first leased it from the feudal lord after he was released from his service as a samurai. In a rare gesture of goodwill—and to signal that there was no dishonor in relieving Jomei of his position—the *daimyo*[2] had rewarded Jomei with the property for his exemplary service. He had even extended an invitation to Jomei and his son, Ichiro, to maintain ties of service with his lordship. But Jomei resigned himself to a life of farming and to teaching what he could to his descendants, however long he might be given to live.

The old man ate a sweet rice cake and sipped from

one of the two cups Aiko had brought without his ever noticing her. His thoughts were otherwise engaged, and she kept a respectful distance.

Suddenly a shadow of sadness moved across Jomei's face. "Please do not say that you have found lodgings elsewhere," Jomei protested. Aware that one cannot restrain the movement of the spirit, he reconsidered and took a different tack. "Perhaps you will take me along on your journey, on the waters, across our sea," he said aloud. "Perhaps," Jomei mumbled to himself, then seemed to concede whatever his guest had said. The visit appeared to continue amicably for some time.

Whatever this strange visit really was, it was blatantly disobedient to the shogun's orders. No foreigners were allowed into the country; likewise no native Japanese were permitted to leave it. In Japan foreigners were barred from almost everywhere, beginning from its outer reaches. Nagasaki was the exception; it coddled foreigners—mostly traders—in its fine warm harbor.

The consensus was that the greatest danger foreigners brought to Japan had nothing to do with commerce or trade. It was their ideas and beliefs which, if left unchecked, could bring unwanted change to well-ordered Japanese society and the powerful men who ruled it. Portuguese missionaries had long been expelled. Those who remained in the interior had been summarily executed in the failed Shimabara rebellion, which had been largely blamed on Christians.

Even before that there had been waves of Christian persecution and extermination in Japan. The great *daimyo* Toyotomi Hideyoshi had outlawed the religion altogether in 1587, forty years after the Jesuit priest Francis Xavier first introduced Christianity to a small gathering of listeners in Kagoshima, also on the island of Kyushu. Succeeding shoguns carried out the ban on Christianity to varying degrees. They did so believing the faith to be a weapon in the hands of foreigners who sought to influence Japan.

Small scattered settlements of Christian converts remained throughout Japan, but nowhere had Christians anchored their roots as deeply as they had in Nagasaki. Even traces of Christian faith were considered dangerous, however, and all its adherents had to be wiped out. This task was assigned to the *daimyos* and their military detachments of samurais. Ridding Japan of Christians did not come easily. Although a few left the country altogether, most never renounced their faith and were executed with gruesome practicality. Nevertheless, there were persistent rumors that a small number of Christians had gone into hiding, particularly in the Nagasaki district of Urakami. The *kakure kirishitan*, or "secret Christians," were referred to in low murmurs among the samurai, who once could have counted a few Christians among themselves.

"Sofu-san!" Aiko whispered to her *ojiisan*,[3] unaware of the unseen guest her grandfather had before him. "I am off to do the wash. Will you be all right here alone?" There was something about her grandfather's behavior that had troubled Aiko all morning. "Mother and Father will be here shortly," she assured him. "Can you manage, Sofu-san?"

On most mornings he was absorbed in his calligraphy, preferring to work without interruption while the rest of the household left him to his thoughts. Aiko was accustomed to being unnoticed whenever her grandfather took a brush in hand. Sometimes, he appeared almost as if he were praying. She excused herself with a low bow and left for the nearby stream. Camellia hedges bordered the house. It would be good to gather a few green branches for the family's ancestral shrine before their white blooms opened in late fall, she thought.

She had just departed when Jomei suddenly called out. "Aiko, Aiko!" The sound of his distress opened a cavern of fear in her heart. As she raced back to the house, the ball of clothes she had clutched under her arms fell forgotten onto the grass. The old man's face was peaceful when she approached him, as if he had just heard some important news he had long been awaiting.

"Aiko," Jomei said. The sound of his speech rose with much difficulty, "Get some water. Hurry, my child."

# Lorenzo Ruiz

# CHAPTER 1

Lorenzo dipped his brush pen in ink and marked the date on his calendar: Tuesday, June 10, 1636. It was the date he was to set sail from the Philippines. Lorenzo had already said goodbye to his three children and his beloved wife, Rosario. He had also asked both his Chinese and Filipino relatives to keep an eye on his family while he was gone.

"Do everything you can to keep Rosario from worrying," he pleaded. But Lorenzo suspected that only his safe return home would put her fears to rest.

Despite the rains and his sad departure, the family shared some early morning cheer: a cup of hot Chinese tea between husband and wife, and a rare treat of ground roasted cacao beans whipped with warmed carabao's[1] milk for the children. The thick aroma of the chocolate filled the room. The cacao beans had come as a gift from the Dominican friars, who had hefty bags of them imported from New Spain[2] in America half a world away.

Lorenzo had a good relationship with the Dominican missionaries. He often thanked God for the many opportunities and blessings that came his way through the Spanish friars. It was from them that Lorenzo and the rest of his

11

family learned about the faith. Moreover, because Lorenzo's penmanship was superb, the Dominicans also helped him develop the skills of a parish recorder—an *escríbano*. Working at the local parish office as a notary scribe, Lorenzo had been able to earn a decent living. And through the Dominicans' special love for the Blessed Virgin Mary, he became deeply devoted to praying the Rosary and was known as a dedicated member of the Confraternity of the Most Holy Rosary.

Looking back, Lorenzo reflected upon the fact that he had lived his whole life under the protection of the Church. Lorenzo was born in humble circumstances around the year 1600 (probably on August 10), of Catholic parents. At his Baptism they named him Lorenzo after Saint Lawrence, a deacon who was martyred in Rome in 258, at the height of early Christian persecution under the Roman emperor Valerian. He was roasted on a red-hot gridiron.

Lorenzo was educated at a Dominican school, but he also benefited from the combined knowledge of his parents, who drew from the richness of their own cultures and experiences. Lorenzo's Filipina mother taught him to speak the native language, Tagalog. His Chinese father taught him to speak Chinese and write in *kanji*, the difficult style of classical Chinese characters.

The summer monsoons had begun late this year. But on the morning of Lorenzo's departure from the Chinese quarter of Manila, it seemed as if the skies were eager to dump a deluge upon them. Not many of the usually numerous vendors moved their boats along the waterways in the torrential rain. But a kind vegetable merchant offered Lorenzo a ride to the wharf at the mouth of the Pásig River. Not once did he ask Lorenzo why he was in such a hurry to get there; nor did he suggest waiting for the rains to subside. The downpour provided an added curtain of safety for Lorenzo, who was uneasy and on edge after the unexpected turn of events within the past weeks. He knew, however, that the rain would not be enough to shield him forever.

As the rains fell, Lorenzo's thoughts drifted back. Not long ago, his days had seemed completely secure. Lorenzo and his family lived in simple joy and breathed a faith that sustained them. Yet he also knew that life would never be trouble-free for a native Filipino under Spanish rule in his own homeland. Other Filipinos had not fared as well as Lorenzo had with the friars or the civil authorities. But those days of contentment felt an eternity away. Everything had changed the instant he had been falsely accused. *A murder?* It was so unjust he could hardly believe it had happened.

Everyone was talking about it: a brawl had broken out between a Spanish ship's mate and a fellow Spaniard. Both had been drinking heavily and the evening had deteriorated. They argued, then one of them pulled out his knife and plunged it into the gut of the other. The victim died on the scene. The other man had staggered away in a drunken haze and evaded capture from the authorities.

"Who will the Spanish arrest?" That was the question whispered on every street corner and in every home. The Spaniards who settled on the numerous Filipino islands numbered barely more than 1 percent of the population. In order for the Spanish to remain in control, they felt it was necessary to rule with an iron hand. Both settlers and natives knew what to expect when a crime was committed. If the victim was a Spaniard, someone *must* be made to answer for the crime. But if the authorities detained an ordinary Spanish drunkard, the execution by hanging would serve little purpose. To strengthen Spain's grip on the Philippines, the authorities felt it was important to punish a local now and then as a warning to everyone.

"Why not search for the real killer?" Lorenzo had suggested. Native witnesses, and the usual odd assortment of false informers and decoys, were hesitant to come forward when it came to testifying against a Spaniard. "Why make up charges against an innocent man?" he asked.

Perhaps it was the boldness of Lorenzo's suggestion, or the fact that it came from a native, that irritated the Spanish law enforcement officials in the city of Manila. With a sense of injured pride, a Spanish officer had been quick to suggest an alternative. "Why not arrest Lorenzo Ruiz as a suspect in the murder of the Spanish soldier? He associates closely with the Dominicans and is half Chinese." Most Spaniards distrusted the Chinese anyway. This fueled the charges against Lorenzo even more. He was, by their account, a particularly convenient scapegoat.

As he wondered about his decision to flee, Lorenzo realized it was the only choice he really had. *Prejudice,* Lorenzo thought, *creates its own criteria. If they can justify false charges, what will stop them from justifying an execution?*

The news spread rapidly. Immediately, the Dominican superior, Father Antonio Gonzales, suggested that Lorenzo leave with them for a religious mission in Japan. This would save his life. The ship was scheduled to make a stop at Formosa, the Portuguese name for Taiwan, where Lorenzo planned to remain. Though the journey would separate him from his family for a time, Lorenzo gratefully agreed. Being half Chinese, he could blend in, find work or a trade, and plan to move his family there in the near future. The separation was only temporary. It would end up being more of a relocation than an escape. In Manila, he was a dead man. It was only a matter of time.

"You only have one life, Lorenzo. We must make whatever sacrifices are necessary to save it. May God help you begin a new life for all of us in Formosa," Rosario said, her voice trembling with emotion.

"And may he soon reunite our family," Lorenzo added, still not quite believing his present dilemma.

*With God, nothing is impossible*, he thought. Still, both of them suspected that this physical separation was only the beginning. There would be more struggle and sacrifice to come before the family would be reunited.

Rosario turned in prayer to the Blessed Mother, and appealed to Our Lady of Sorrows to strengthen, protect, and intercede for them. For now, she would have to raise their three children without her husband.

Falsely accused, troubled, and uncertain, Lorenzo offered a simple and straightforward prayer—one of trust. "Jesus, give me faith. You once said to your disciples that if any of them had faith the size of a tiny mustard seed, it would be enough to move mountains. My departure is a heavy cross for us to bear. Help us."

Help us to escape? Help us to fight back? No. What mattered increasingly to Lorenzo was what God willed, and not what Lorenzo himself wanted because of his fears. In his uneventful daily life he had seen it many times: carrying out God's will always brought about a greater good than achieving one's own desires. The difficulty was finding and discerning God's will. There was the obvious will of God, Lorenzo knew, that was found in the Ten Commandments he had learned as a child. But Lorenzo also knew that there is sometimes a greater calling: to give oneself totally to God, to reach true freedom by embracing God's will fully.

Lorenzo began to perceive that God was taking him to places he would rather not go. He did not *want* to leave his family, but Lorenzo also felt that God was leading him to take this step for the good of all. This brief boat ride, soaked in monsoon rains, was just the first leg of the journey. Although it may have appeared insignificant to others, Lorenzo understood that his actions were a real sacrifice for both himself and his small family. Placed in the heart of God, every moment of this separation would have meaning and lasting value.

Squinting into the future, Lorenzo realized that he was on a path of sorrow, a *via dolorosa*—his way of the cross. His soul's inner regions of fear and oppression, pain and anxiety, desolation and darkness would culminate on his very own Mount Calvary. But with crucifixion would also come resurrection. The promise of liberation from death and of eternal life would be fulfilled in a decisive victory without end. He would then bring his family to Formosa and all would be well.

"No one can impose God's will on me," Lorenzo whispered to himself. "It is something I want to carry out freely, just as the Blessed Virgin did." *Hail Mary, full of grace, the Lord is with you* . . . The beads of the rosary slipped through his fingers.

All this occupied Lorenzo's thoughts as the boat made its way to the Boca del Rio Pásig. Dressed in pantaloons and capped with a tattered sombrero, Lorenzo joined some native fishermen. They sailed past the Spanish garrison and across the bay to Cavite unnoticed; then the colossal galleon[3] berthed at the pier came into view.

A few dried-fish merchants helped load an array of foodstuff and provisions into the vessel's hold. It would have to provide enough supplies for the voyage across the passages of southern Luzon and into the treacherous Strait of San Bernardino. Some galleons, failing to make it beyond that to the Pacific, crashed instead against rock formations and splintered into wreckage. But if they reached the open sea, the ship would catch the trade winds and head north to Formosa. *This is my best chance for freedom*, thought Lorenzo.

At best, it would be another two weeks before Lorenzo would set foot on land again. But as he approached the ship, Lorenzo realized that he would have to find a way to board it undetected. Checkpoints had been set up to monitor the movement of natives. To the soldiers who manned them, Lorenzo was a wanted man on the run.

# The Voyage

# CHAPTER 2

Lorenzo knew he must board the galleon quickly. He hoisted the instruments of his trade onto his shoulders: a portable wooden desk with storage for his pens and ink blocks. He also carried a change of clothing and other necessities, food, and a jumble of wares packed with care in a rectangular wicker case. From a distance he might have been mistaken for any of the toiling longshoremen and stevedores[1] shuttling to and from the galleons, backs bowed with heavy loads and overstuffed luggage. But up close, Lorenzo's uncalloused hands and lighter skin might betray him.

Without so much as a glance at the ship's notary, who positioned himself at a small table down the boarding plank, Lorenzo grabbed hold of some large freight tethers and clambered onto the ship. His agile move had the added benefit of making Lorenzo look like he had worked on a ship all his life and thus avoiding the illegal passport fee that the ship's notary swindled from other inexperienced passengers.

As Lorenzo finally alighted on deck he heard from below the familiar bellow of Father Antonio's baritone voice. Lorenzo could see the portly friar pointing one accusing finger and then another at the ship's notary. The notary had barred him and the other Dominicans from boarding until they coughed up enough pesos for the supposed passport fee. Lorenzo watched, and listened.

"One silver peso each," the notary announced firmly.

"Should I quote our great Spanish poet, Miguel de Cervantes, and what he had to say about *escríbanos* such as yourself, my good friend?"

"Tell me, friar. But your words will not stop me," the notary replied with disinterest.

"There are many good, faithful and legal recorders . . . and not all of them exact excessive fees for their services," quoted Father Antonio.

"*Excessive*, Padre? It's a mere token from all your collections that keep you in such fine form," the *escríbano* interjected, pointing at Father Antonio's thick waistline.

"I won't pay this fee, nor will I stand for such insults!" Father Antonio roared. "In fact I will take this matter up with the ship's master and captain, both of whom I know very well, for I baptized the one and confirmed the other."

"Forgive me, Father," the *escríbano* mumbled, scratching his head under his red cap.

The other Dominican friars carefully made their way around Father Antonio and proceeded up the plank to board the ship. Father Antonio grumbled one more time.

"Let's not lose our good humor, Padre. We have a few weeks to spend together aboard the *San Lorenzo*. I'll get that fee from you yet, if not in this life then most certainly in the next," the Spanish *escríbano* teased. "Give unto Caesar what is Caesar's, Padre." Father Antonio was fuming, so much so that he failed to hear the *escríbano's* last words as he moved on.

Lorenzo walked stealthily around the ship. He usually saw the sailing galleons gliding into the bay of Manila from afar. The ship on which the friars had secured passage was providentially named after Lorenzo's patron saint. Perhaps it was only an eerie coincidence. No one would deny, however, that the *San Lorenzo* was something to behold. With more than seven hundred tons of cargo space, it was one of the largest and most majestic ships in the service of the Spanish crown. The Spaniards had been building ships larger and larger. Some argued the bigger they came the more difficult they were to maneuver on the water.

In truth, the galleons were graceful vessels and could be operated without much difficulty by a relatively small number of men. The *San Lorenzo* had a crew of thirty-five Spaniards, not counting the thirty native Filipinos aboard who were forced into service.

Other galleons bobbed in the water beside the *San Lorenzo*. Together they would form a convoy of three ships on the journey, a small *flota*, or fleet. The Spanish preferred sailing in groups to discourage the all too common pirate attacks. Trade in the Far East was also fiercely competitive; Dutch and the English privateers posed the leading threat to Spanish commerce.

The galleons were scheduled to sail to Formosa for trade with the ever-present Dutch, who had established a commercial base there with the Chinese. From Formosa the *San Lorenzo* would voyage to Okinawa, to further trade with the Japanese. Chinese goods—mostly silks, elaborate textiles, ivory, porcelains, spices, even beeswax and gold—were then shipped across the Pacific to New Spain, where the galleons anchored in the city of Acapulco. The trip spanned some four to five months on the open ocean, one way, provided the ships did not hit the doldrums. Many attested that the return trip proved much swifter and lasted only three to four months. In any case the round trip from Manila to Acapulco and back kept the crew away from home for a year.

Native Filipinos were often forced into mandatory service without any contract for their labor on these ships. Their names were not even written in the ships' registers, as if their presence aboard was completely without significance. Some had been forced into servitude in place of imprisonment, but there was little difference between those options. Some Filipinos, if they made it to the western shore of New Spain alive, would escape. Others—starved, overworked, and abused—died along the journey. A few were killed; some even threw themselves overboard to end their miseries.

And yet among the Spanish, the Chinese, and native Filipinos there were those who thrived on this kind of life. For them, the lure of adventure on the sea outweighed the safety and security offered by toil on land. Those who survived more than one voyage lived a hardened existence of exposure to the elements. They slept on deck when the weather was fair or mildly inclement. Otherwise they found lodgings on the lower decks. Rats and roaches multiplied in the maze of crevices between the ship and crates of goods. Lorenzo saw that the sailors' complexion turned leathery from the spray of salt water. Their eyes were red from melancholy, resignation, and malnutrition. Withdrawn from the world, they spoke very little.

From the height of the main deck Lorenzo could see most of the pier and the numerous businesses that surrounded it. Multiple laundry and tailor shops dotted the road because all travelers and sailors needed decent clothing after making it back to shore. There were also eateries—favored among the local sailors—and restaurants, where Spanish officers and merchants, when not bound in haggling with Chinese merchants for the wholesale purchase of their luxury goods, dined and exchanged fine conversation with comrades. Lastly, the aroma of freshly baked bread and sweet biscuits or cookies that permeated the humid atmosphere enticed all toward the bakeries. These drew both those with a sweet tooth and street children who came begging for crumbs when they were not picking through garbage on the trash heaps mounding close to shore.

He met Father Antonio at the ship's well, the middle portion of the main deck that separated the rear or aftercastle[2] from the forward prow. Only on the rare occasion did Lorenzo ever experience the full force of the friar's anger, and that had been when he was still in training for the job of parish notary.

"Oh, ho, Lorenzo," the good friar's mood changed as swiftly as the retracting leaves of the native *makahiya* plant. "You made it, you made it! Very well, will you take these to our quarters?" he asked, handing Lorenzo some of his belongings straightaway. "But afterward you may have to bunk with the crew. No bed, you understand, just wherever you can find to lay your head without getting in the way."

"Certainly, Father. I am just glad to be aboard."

"Good. It's your first time on a galleon, isn't it? Well, it can be quite *interesting*, to say the least," he said in an easy tone. "But you'll see for yourself. If you've never had a strong stomach before," he said pointing to his own belly, "you will have one after this trip, I can assure you. Now, go and keep yourself busy until I speak to the ship's master and the captain." Then rather conspiratorially he added, "Should anyone ask, you are our sacristan—as you truly are—all right?"

"Yes, Padre." But just as Lorenzo turned away, he heard the anxiety in Father Antonio's voice.

"*Ay, Dios mío*, forgive us, forgive us all our sins," he said while looking out from the deck to the coastline. "And help us make the sacrifices we'll have to make to atone for all of our shortcomings."

Lorenzo's traveling companions included the three European Dominican priests: Father Antonio Gonzalez and Father Miguel de Aozaraza, both Spaniards, as well as Father Guillermo Courtet, a Frenchman of noble birth. Also with them, however, was a Japanese priest, Father Vicente Shiwozuka de la Cruz. Japanese priests were rare, but not unheard-of in the Philippines. Most, like Father Vicente, worked with Christian Japanese exiles in Manila. Last among the travelers was a Japanese layman, a leper, called Lazaro of Kyoto. Lazaro's limbs and parts of his face were wasted away from the incurable disease. It was almost as if the leprosy had set out to erase Lazaro's identity as a human being. Though expelled from his homeland, he was an educated man and a Christian. Fluent in Japanese and Spanish, Lazaro of Kyoto would serve as a translator for Father Antonio on this missionary enterprise to preach the Good News to the people of Japan.

All were aboard and they waited, as the journey did not commence immediately. In fact, depending on the winds and the weather and a myriad of other considerations on the ship's master's checklist, it could be another two days or more before the ship set sail for Formosa. With the loading and transferring of cargo to balance the vessel and all it took to secure the necessary foodstuff and passengers, Lorenzo realized he could have held on to his family at least a day longer. His own words to his wife, Rosario, echoed in his mind. *We cannot be burdened by our fears and sentiments.* Now Lorenzo was discovering just how difficult it would be to listen to his own stern counsel.

# CHAPTER 3

Lorenzo opened the door and entered respectfully into the priests' quarters, wiping his feet at the threshold before gently releasing Father Antonio's luggage. He noticed a crucifix on a heavily ornamented base had already been placed on a small table. *Perhaps this is the chaplain's cabin.*

"Lorenzo," Father Guillermo's voice, with his subtle French accent, startled him. "Leave your own things in here as well if you don't want them stolen by the crew," he advised. "And if you need a cape, Father Miguel can give you one of his."

"I can?" Father Miguel chuckled. "But it'll cost you, Lorenzo, maybe half your lunch ration, perhaps for the entire journey," he teased.

"Most certainly not. Now don't think all Basques are stingy and wily, Lorenzo," Father Guillermo countered. "This one has been converted by yours truly and I can assure you he is willing to share what he has."

"What *I* have? What about what *you* have?" Father Miguel argued. "Don't believe these French clerics, Lorenzo. They tell *you* to share but spare nothing from their own pockets or suitcases. Now, to show you that I am true to my

Basque heritage and Father Guillermo is a true Frenchman, I will give you *his* cape for the journey. May it keep you warm."

Father Miguel handed Lorenzo a warm woolen cape, but Lorenzo was unsure if the gesture was in good humor or not. The friars studied his reaction and smiled broadly. "Go on, take it," Father Guillermo encouraged. "We poke fun to remind ourselves that the journey need not be tedious."

"Yes," assured Father Miguel. "The cape is yours, Lorenzo. It's new and our gift to you, especially because you will be out there with the crew and it can get chilly and damp at night." The cabin in which the priests would stay for the duration of the voyage was small; there was barely enough space for their belongings on the floor. Father Miguel took the top bunk, where the rocking of the ship was more noticeably felt. He left the lower bed for the older and less agile Father Antonio.

"Thank you," Lorenzo said gratefully. "Now I feel and look like a real sailor." He hung the cape over his arm as if he were a gentleman's servant.

"And if it gets rough out there, you can stay here with us in our quarters . . ." Father Antonio's offer was sincere.

" . . . or here with us in ours," the Japanese priest, Father Vicente, added. He and Lazaro of Kyoto were separated by a cloth curtain in their cabin. This was the best remedy the ship's captain could manage, a kind of flimsy quarantine to prevent the contagion of leprosy aboard ship.

"Thank you, Fathers," Lorenzo said. "I plan to do what I can to avoid any problems so that I can blend in with the rest of the crew. Besides, it's my chance to see how my Filipino brothers fare in their work here."

"A wise decision," Father Miguel said. "But have your meals with us. You owe me that portion of your ration after all, a great big lump of beans and rice and salt pork." He smacked his lips in mock appreciation.

"Oh, Father, from the sound of it, you would have it all," Lorenzo snapped back.

"You learn fast, dear brother," said Father Guillermo. "Before the end of this trip, you will be bantering with the best of us."

"But wait . . . I just had a good idea," said Father Miguel, smelling something interesting. "Perhaps you can cook something more palatable for us instead of the usual ship's fare?" They all gave the idea an approving nod. "And why not? The captain always lacks a good cook on these voyages. It seems to me that when the cook displeases the crew, it's off with him," said Father Miguel.

"Well, I can cook if my life depends on it," Lorenzo countered. "And I can share the leftovers with all of you, I suppose." That got a round of applause from the small gathering of religious. "That *is* a good idea, Father Miguel," said Lorenzo. "Maybe I should offer my services to the crew through Father Antonio."

"There's no need to tell me," Father Antonio said, huffing as he came up the ladder to the *toldilla*.[1] "You've already been assigned by the ship's captain, Don Enrique, to manage the galley for us during the trip—specifically the cooking. Nothing fancy, just that quick toss of the ingredients that you do so well, Lorenzo."

"Yes, Father Antonio. I'll try."

"Very well, present yourself to the captain. He is in his quarters," Father Antonio directed.

Lorenzo stood for a second, wondering if he should go alone.

"Go on, son. Don't be afraid. There are more things to fear than introducing yourself to the ship's captain. This is not the time for timid nerves."

As Lorenzo made his way down to the captain's quarters, Father Guillermo spoke quietly in confidence to Father Antonio.

"Do you think you should've at least sent one of us to accompany him to meet the captain?"

"No," Father Antonio said. "Lorenzo is a good servant. He does as he's told. But on this ship, he has to be his own man. That's why I advised him to stay with the crew and get a taste of what life is like aboard ship. In a way, we've sheltered him. But before we disembark he will have been tried in countless ways that we can't foresee aboard a journey like this. I tell you, though, he won't be found lacking in faith."

"Yes, but he is already separated from his family," Father Guillermo reasoned.

"Then he will discover that there is a larger family to which he also belongs," Father Antonio said, raising his hand as a signal to cease further discussion.

"Amen, Father. Amen to that," said Father Guillermo, returning to his quarters a bit pensive for having been reproved.

"That may be the result for all of us," Father Antonio said to himself as he shut the makeshift door behind him.

Lorenzo didn't need any help locating the captain's quarters. From the intricately carved wooden doors alone, Lorenzo knew he was entering what amounted to the royal chambers of the ship. Bolts of silk stood end-to-end outside the quarters, and richly embroidered red, gold, and silver apparel hung on racks by the entrance like priceless drapery.

"It's silly to wear a wig in this climate, don't you agree?" asked the captain of Lorenzo as he saw him by the doorway. "Come in, come in," he motioned with two forefingers as he rubbed the sweat off his head with the other hand.

Lorenzo entered and stood before the captain, cape in arm and hat to his chest.

"I am Lorenzo Ruiz, your excellency," he bowed.

"No need for formalities, Lorenzo, and I am no "excellency." Father Antonio tells me you can cook, and well. That will be your job aboard ship four days of the week. If your meals are good, we will let you cook every day. We'll try out your cooking on the crew first, and if they survive, you can include the rest of us. Go and see the officers' cook and he will give you more instructions. Do you have any questions?"

"None, Don Enrique."

"Very well, you may take your leave."

" . . . except that, what if my cooking is not to the crew's liking?"

"Ah, then," laughed the captain, "It's off with you, isn't it?"

# CHAPTER 4

Lorenzo made his way back down to the main deck, where the ship's stove was located in a sandbox so as to minimize the chance of starting a fire that would imperil the whole ship. People were milling about noisily. Not quite sure what to do next, he stood there like a forlorn chef, without utensils and cooking accessories, until one of the ship's crew approached him.

"Idiot! Who stands there in the middle of the ship like that? You're in the way. Do you want to get yourself killed?"

"I am looking for the officers' cook. Do you know where I can find him?"

"Who wants to know?"

"The captain, Don Enrique, sent me," Lorenzo replied, a bit shaken.

"And why would he send you, *Indio*?"

Knowing that the term *Indio*—literally "Indian"— was a derogatory term among the Spaniards, Lorenzo simply replied, "I am the cook for the crew."

At this the commotion around Lorenzo ceased for a moment and a hail of laughter battered his ears.

"The crew has a cook now?" the man asked rather cynically. "Why? What's the matter? The last cook was not good enough so they send us another one we'll only throw overboard as well? We cook for ourselves, *Indio*. Do you think we trust you with our rations?" The others joined in the jeering until the boatswain dispersed them all with a sharp blow on his whistle. Lorenzo's hearing was momentarily impaired.

"What do you want, *Indio*?" asked the boatswain. "I am Carlos. But to you, it's Don Carlos, *¿comprendes?*"

Lorenzo nodded.

"I don't understand nods. In some places here it means 'yes,' in others, 'no.' With me you speak up, *¿entiendes?*"

"*Sí*, Don Carlos," Lorenzo answered quietly.

"Forget it. I know you are the cook. Remember, impress us or else. . . . Now, you are looking for Giuseppe. He's the officers' cook. You report to him, *¿entiendes?* He's on the second deck bodega, the ship's storage area, minding the firewood. Tell him to get his butt up here because the firewood is going nowhere, the lazy bum."

"Yes, sir," Lorenzo responded as he turned to leave. Uncertain of how he would manage to deliver such a message, he wove his way through the decks in search of Giuseppe.

Lorenzo passed the cannons on both gun decks, where some of the crew bunked and slept on the floors in between the cannons. When he finally reached the second deck bodega, Lorenzo called out for Giuseppe. There was no reply. He noticed that the Filipino crew was handling the storage of cargo in the lower decks. They looked at Lorenzo with mild surprise, but none of them said anything to him.

A disturbance of sorts was brewing in the first deck, which lay half beneath water level. Lorenzo continued his descent. There were no portholes on these decks, just darkness pockmarked by faint light from glass-covered lanterns. The lowest level of storehouse lay in these parts. Standing water had already turned the atmosphere stale, and the aroma of mold mixed with tar made for a sickening combination. Only *Indio* eyes gleamed in this netherworld.

Here the water pipes reached down from the main deck, from which water was siphoned and pumped up to prevent the ship from sinking. Lorenzo felt as if he had reached into the very gut of a big whale. But he did not entertain any further thought of being a Jonah of his day.

"Hey you, *estúpido*, what do you think you're doing down there?" someone called out from the deck above.

For a split second Lorenzo was amazed that his ears had not yet fallen off from all the insults, foul language, and curses he had already encountered on board the ship.

"I was sent to find Giuseppe."

"Who wants to know?" the man asked.

"I am Lorenzo, his new assistant until we reach Formosa."

"Why? What's in Formosa?"

"That's where I get off," Lorenzo answered.

"I see, and what can you do?"

"I can cook—in the native Filipino way and in the Chinese style," Lorenzo said.

"Hah. Where did you learn this?"

"From my father and mother," Lorenzo called out from the first deck cavern. "And from my wife—she cooks, too." A momentary pause eclipsed the line of questioning and filled Lorenzo's heart with longing for home. *How are Rosario and the children doing without me?* he wondered.

"All right, then, *I* am Giuseppe," the man said, reaching out a muscled arm to help Lorenzo up the ladder. "And I would appreciate it if you do not mistake me for any of the

Spaniards because I am not one of *them*. Even better, I am Italian. That boatswain upstairs who thinks he can intimidate me, he is part German. And the ship's master, who gossips about everything to the captain, is Portuguese." Lorenzo detected his new supervisor's cultural pride and was appreciative of the tidbits of information he shared.

"Next to the captain—and even with him I reserve my doubts—I am the only one who knows about fine food and cuisine," Giuseppe boasted. "You know, we Italians have ruled the world for centuries. You know this, right?" he said as he flicked the back of his hand on Lorenzo's chest. "Now we have to put up with these ruffians. Hah! I laugh at them. The world is round and one day you are at the top," he said, drawing an arc with his index fingers, "and another you are at the bottom. Soon they will be where they don't want or expect to be. And what about you? What were you before the Spanish came along?"

Lorenzo smiled at his wise and articulate philosopher-chef. "We were—"

"Never mind. I already know . . . you were . . . neither here nor there, probably having a good time anyway, right? That is, until the Spanish showed up and ruined it all for you, yes?" he nudged Lorenzo. "Yes?" His eyes twinkled as he shot Lorenzo a knowing look, "Hmmm, Lamberto?"

"It's *Lorenzo*, sir, like the ship." Lorenzo spoke gently, but Giuseppe turned on him in a flash.

"You are whatever I call you, friend. If it's Lamberto, you say, '*sí*.' If it's Luciano, Luigi, or Leonardo, you reply only '*sí*.' Understand, my friend?"

"*Sí*," Lorenzo whispered, lowering his eyes. He realized immediately the importance of this lesson about life on a galleon. Giuseppe was not cruel, but these Europeans were not like the Dominican priests who had helped him escape. To them, he was only a poor native. There would be no banter. Boldness in an *Indio* was not welcome.

It was easy for emotions to become enflamed aboard ship over the pettiest matters. Space on the vessel came at a premium and those with any rank, however minor, guarded their territories with a vicious possessiveness he had never encountered before.

"The sailors are quick to draw their knives," Giuseppe warned him, "so don't get into any arguments with them."

Lorenzo discovered, however, that it was easy enough to get along, as long as he agreed with whomever he was talking to. At every turn he found himself offering a short prayer for whomever he met, and made the best of his situation. Still, Lorenzo worried about his family—and missed them terribly. The ship hadn't even left port yet.

"The worst thing you can experience on a ship is a storm," Giuseppe lectured as they prepared the foodstuffs and provisions in the bodega and the forward prow. "It demoralizes everyone.

"There is no reliable way to predict the weather," he continued. "Whatever the ship's pilot glimpses on the horizon, is what we will meet."

Lorenzo set another heavy sack down. "We can pray for a safe passage, and ask the Virgin Mary, the Star of the Sea, to guide those who maneuver the ship. Jesus calmed a storm at sea," Lorenzo said. Giuseppe just looked at him.

"Yes," Giuseppe responded. "You would think that the best season to cross the oceans would be when the waters are calm. But sailors do not prefer calm seas," he said, his voice getting louder. "Ships cannot advance with speed without the propelling movement of the wind. And wind causes waves. Therefore sailors depend on turbulent seas. And we will share their fate."

Pulling Lorenzo aside, Giuseppe warned that they would be preparing heavy meals for the crew in the event of a storm so they all could eat well while they could eat at all. With everyone manning his station to prevent the ship from sinking, the next meal might not be for two days.

In addition to cooking, Lorenzo and Giuseppe also scrubbed decks, inventoried the food supplies, and sometimes, even cleaned the latrine.

Their well-being, already precarious in times of pestilence and natural disaster, became still more fragile at sea. "I tell you," Giuseppe groaned, "not only do we have to worry about what goes in here," he pointed to his mouth, but we must also worry about what goes out from there," he said, pointing to his backside and shaking his head in disgust. "If our food makes the crew ill, there are no guarantees about what any of them might do to us."

The weekly menu included assigned meals for the days of the week. Sunday and Thursday meals, for instance, were the same and offered the crew biscuits or rice, a liter of water, a liter of wine, a pound of salted pork or sausage and a small two-ounce cube of cheese. Other days saw some variation; some days the crew had salted fish or sardines, and on others beans and salted meat (salt being the best way to preserve food).[1] At times there was not enough water to quench their thirst after a salty meal.

During storms, though, food was kept at a minimum and included only bread, cheese, and wine. No one would fire up the stoves on deck, if at all possible, when everything was drenched.

Giuseppe instructed Lorenzo that only officers ate on a table, in the captain's quarters. The crew, instead, used their storage chests to sit on or to eat on in the forward prow. And their food came heaped in platters, where all shared in the portions. Whoever came last sopped up whatever was left with his ration of rice and biscuit. Lunch was the heaviest meal of the day, but smaller rations were given during the doldrums when the weather was calm, and during storms.

"If a cook is enterprising enough," Giuseppe said, "he could make extra money aboard by scrimping on the rations and selling them back to the crew for a profit. Although," he warned, "this is what upset the crew on past voyages and why they were justified in throwing the cook off the ship." Lorenzo listened, trying to make sense of it. "For me," said Giuseppe, "it served no purpose to act so cruelly. That's why I arranged for them to pay me extra to be honest from the start, before the voyage. No misunderstandings at sea!" he said grinning.

*All this food talk seems fine and good for Giuseppe,* Lorenzo thought, *but what about the others?* Lorenzo asked, "What about the rest of the crew? What about the Filipino crew?"

"They eat whenever and whatever. Their meals are always scraps, really," Giuseppe said matter-of-factly. "But this is the same as where I come from. I started out this way, you know? A page at eight years old. How can a boy fight grown men when they go hungry? You wait and see, my friend. The *Indio* crew, they do the same." He shrugged his shoulders as if everything were settled.

By the morning of the tenth, a Tuesday, the ship's pilot had advised the captain that the opportune time of departure had arrived. All crew members stood on deck, as was the custom. The ship's officers dressed in their formal array. The friars stood with their hands clasped together, heads bowed and ready for the opening prayer. With the rise of the tide, the ropes were hauled in, and the anchors raised.

# CHAPTER 5

With a single nod from the captain, the ship's master signaled the boatswain to cast off. Don Carlos blew his whistle—a rather forlorn beginning to the launch. Then the ship's chaplain, Father Antonio, led an invocation: "Ease the rope of the foresail, in the name of the Father, and Son and Holy Spirit, three persons in one true God, that he may be with us and give us a good and safe voyage. May he carry us and return us safely to our homes!" he said, to which all the ship's crew resounded in unison, "Amen."[1]

Nothing had prepared Lorenzo for the spectacle of the unfurling of the sails. Each of the five masts carried as many as three huge sails. The main mast stood in the center, with the two huge, square sails one on top of the other and a smaller one at the crest. And crowning the grouping, the Spanish flag in the royal colors of red and yellow flapped sharply in the breeze. To Lorenzo the galleon resembled a crescent moon riding below a billowy cloud of canvas. It was likely the grandest and most beautiful thing he had ever seen.

From the eastern fringes of the South China Sea, the galleon made its way south and then turned due southeast back into Philippine waterways. The pilot, Don Alfonso, would navigate the *San Lorenzo* around various Philippine islands until it reached the farthest eastern limit—the San Bernardino Strait. A magnificent though narrow threshold to the Pacific, there was a small island in the middle of it where the final *embarcadero* or wharf would be found. Whatever replenishment of fresh water or coconuts could be had, this final *embarcadero* was the last opportunity for days on end. The crew talked about passing through the strait and into the open sea with both reverence and apprehension. Locals on board maintained their own ancient myths and superstitions, but also appealed to Our Lady of Good Voyage for protection.

Before sunset, just after the three o'clock prayer, the last meal of the day was served aboard ship. Shortly afterward, the fire from the hearth had to be put out before nightfall as a matter of precaution.

"It's the lull before the storm," said Giuseppe.

"How do you know?" asked Lorenzo.

"I can smell it, my friend," he answered, flicking the tip of his nose with his index finger.

Giuseppe manned the galley as Lorenzo served the officers and the friars, who sat at the captain's table as his guests. Father Miguel made a gesture of approval for the cuisine. Most of the crew preferred to do their own cooking. But Lorenzo managed to whip up some *pancit* for the Filipinos aboard—a typical dish of sautéed rice noodles and whatever leftovers were available. The effort won him a few new *Indio* friends.

One Filipino in particular introduced himself as "Guapo," the Spanish word for "handsome," yet in this case it was a nickname that amounted to an acknowledgement of his unkempt appearance.

*"Pag naitaas na lahat ng mga layag, nasa malaking*

*dagat na tayo*—when all the sails are raised, we will be fully out to sea," Guapo said in Tagalog, the native tongue. "*Salamat sa luto niyo*—thanks for the meal."

"*Walang anuman*—you're welcome," Lorenzo replied. Guapo made a rotating glance at the heavens above him and breathed in a last gulp of fresh air before descending to his station below deck.

The movement of the tides fascinated Lorenzo, probably more so because unlike the few islanders who lived in Biri, the northernmost island in Samar province, he had not observed the ocean currents quite so closely before. No one knew—not even any of the Spanish navigators— what caused the tide flows.

"There is no one yet who understands what causes these tidal actions," said Father Vicente, the Japanese Dominican priest.

"What was that, Father?" Lorenzo asked, surfacing from his moment of contemplation.

"You seem to be very absorbed in thought, Lorenzo. What I said was that no one yet understands the reasons for why the tides move as they do—rising and falling, flowing and ebbing. You have certainly heard of the German astronomer Johannes Kepler? He attributes tidal action to the moon, but Galileo disagrees."

"The tides are like the breathing of the ocean if you ask me," Lorenzo said.

"Well put, Lorenzo. And quite poetic, too."

"I don't think of myself as a poet, Father."

"Perhaps you might have wondered about becoming a religious—even a priest—sometime in the not too distant past?" Father Vicente probed.

"No, Father. You know that is not an option for us Filipinos. But I see that the Church has been more open to you Japanese." Lorenzo, though not bitter, became sad.

Religious vocations were not encouraged among the native Filipino people for the time being. Despite the fact that he was happily married and had three children, it had not escaped Lorenzo that his ties to the Dominicans brought him the closest that any *Indio* Filipino could come to assuming the life of a religious. *How much longer must we Filipinos wait to see one of us dedicated to the priesthood?* It was, as far as Lorenzo was concerned, long overdue.

"There is a time for everything under the sun, Lorenzo." It felt as if Father Vicente had heard Lorenzo's thoughts.

"Ecclesiastes," Lorenzo pointed out somberly.

"Qoheleth," Giuseppe interjected through a grumble. "The wisdom of Qoheleth." They laughed lightly at his eavesdropping.

"There will certainly be Filipino priests in the future, Lorenzo, and soon, too, I hope. The situation for nurturing the faith is precarious in Japan. Perhaps what you need now is patience."

"Patience and perhaps the blood of martyrs," Lorenzo added, reminded of how Japanese converts were quick to lay down their lives for the faith.

At that, Father Vicente began to tell the story of the first twenty-six martyrs of Japan, brave souls who died in Nagasaki in 1597. "They were crucified on a hill overlooking the city of Nagasaki and the bay," he said, a reflective distance in his voice. "Some were children. One was as young as twelve years old. There was, though, a connection to Manila," he said. "Many of those who were executed had come as missionaries from the Philippines."

Lorenzo listened intently. Father Vicente recounted how Japanese converts had asked the Manila missions to send over priests, Franciscans in particular, to help visit the faithful throughout the islands of Kyushu and Honshu. They found it increasingly difficult to minister to the growing church themselves, however, after the shogun—the military leader, Toyotomi Hideyoshi—had exiled the missionaries in 1587. After a brief period of religious tolerance, there began a fresh persecution against Christians. This persecution was worse than anything Christians in Japan had experienced before. The first accused Christians were eventually arrested; their faces were mutilated and their bodies tortured along the 497-mile journey over land and sea from Osaka to Nagasaki.

All of the condemned forgave their executioners. One Japanese religious brother named Paul Miki prayed for his captors. "Following Christ's example, I forgive my persecutors," he said. "I do not hate them. I ask God to have pity on all, and I hope my blood will fall on my fellow men as a fruitful rain." It was also said that while hanging on the cross, a priest, Father Peter Baptist, intoned the "Te Deum" until all of the rest of the condemned sang in unison to their death. Such stories did not merely capture Lorenzo's imagination on this long voyage; they inspired his soul.

As he finished telling the story, Father Vicente closed his eyes and hummed the first few notes to the hymn, which he and Lorenzo then offered together in full voice to honor the martyrs of Japan.

> We praise you, God
> We acknowledge you as Lord.
> As the eternal Father
> All the earth venerates you.
> To you all the angels
> To you the heavens and all the powers
> To you the cherubim and seraphim
> Sing with unending voice
> Holy, holy, holy
> Lord God of hosts

Heaven and earth are full
of the majesty of your glory.

The last verse rose and swelled like the deep waters beneath them.

May your mercy be upon us, O Lord,
Since we have hoped in you.
I have hoped in you, O Lord
May I not be confounded forever.

"The martyrs had incredible inner strength," Father Vicente said after a considerable silence. "I only pray that we, by God's grace, might possess but a fraction of their courage."

During his after-dinner stroll Father Antonio Gonzalez joined the two on deck and said, "It is time for vespers."

The two weeks they would spend together sailing to Formosa promised to be the most intense period of prayer that Lorenzo had ever experienced. He remembered hearing the friars pray before but hadn't realized just how much their lives were centered on prayer. Here on deck Lorenzo saw a more complete picture. The friars prayed from sunrise to sunset and then again in the middle of the night. Eight times a day they gathered to offer praise and thanksgiving to the Lord, to intercede for the world and the salvation of souls. Lorenzo, serving as a ship's cook, joined as he was able, and prayed always for his wife and children.

Before killing off the flames from the firebox, deck hands lit a few lamps from it. The captain's quarters already seemed aglow with a soft light inside. The rest of the men stood vigil over the sun's fading light. A storm hurtling far off in the remote distance, just as Giuseppe had sensed, made the rays appear more elongated over the horizon. The day was turning, the tide low.

"Because we stand here in the Far East, let us train our glance westward, to face the holy cities of Jerusalem and Rome, as we pray," Father Antonio suggested, "though we know that God is everywhere."

The band of Dominican friars reassembled on deck, some toting small musical instruments under their arms. Father Miguel, the youngest of them at thirty-eight, carried a *zanfona*, a stringed instrument quite in vogue in Spain. Don Enrique, the captain, had a number of fine musical instruments stored in his quarters and offered them for the friars' use while on this trip.

Father Guillermo took the reed wind instrument and blew an accompanying tune. And the ship's gunner gladly joined the duo with strums from his baroque Spanish guitar. They played and sang until the darkness settled into the crevices of the ship and its creaking boards strained to the accompaniment. Overhead the light of the planet Venus gleamed in the sky beside Polaris—the North Star. By the time they had navigated the first waves of the interisland passage, it was the last quarter of the moon. The stars appeared even brighter beside the thin crescent.

When they concluded prayers some deck hands commenced nibbling at the remaining evidence of food on the platters and sopped up the gravy or sauce with *pan de sal*. If they had not, the rats aboard would have had their share of it. The bread rolls seemed relatively fresh. In a few days they would be stale or crawling with maggots. But whatever leftovers they had would still be eaten. The voyage was young. The bodegas were well stocked, so all ate well, including the Filipino sailors. And neither were they pestered by lice or fleas and other parasites on their bodies, at least not yet.

Their bellies were full and the night was as delicate as the moths that flitted around their lamps. But such niceties barely lasted for more than a few switches of the hour glass because nature surrounded them with unforgiving uncertainties.

It was not long before the motion of the sea began making the men sick. One or two of them began vomiting what they had eaten into buckets. Soon a whole chorus followed them. Seasickness accompanied a "fainting spell."[1] It happened every time sailors went back to sea. It didn't really matter how experienced they were; there was always the possibility of getting seasick. They often said, "The motion of the sea wears you out." How true it was, Lorenzo thought, and it wasn't long before he himself began heaving over the rails on the main deck, too. It was worse than Lorenzo had anticipated. The combination of seasickness further complicated by homesickness put Lorenzo out of commission for three days. In the meantime, they were plying the route of the inner passage, heading toward the final *embarcadero* and the open sea. The sailor's cape from the good friars kept Lorenzo warm, especially as he broke into a cold sweat with every heaving episode. It left him and some others listless by turns until finally they got their sea legs and adjusted to the constant motion. The friars fared no differently. Giuseppe, however, remained strong on his feet even though his stomach was as unsettled as anyone's. "Some fine assistant *you* are," he said to seasick Lorenzo in between feeding him spoonfuls of plain broth.

"If there is a time for seasickness, this is it," Giuseppe proclaimed. "Better to suffer it now, before we pass the San Bernardino Strait. When we reach the open sea the ship will need a full deck of sailors to man the stations."

# CHAPTER 6

Excitement on board rose steadily in anticipation of the San Bernardino crossing. By the time they reached it, the passage seemed to be less dangerous than what anyone had previously expected. Perhaps this was because the tide was ebbing and the waters flowed out to the ocean instead of inward toward the galleon. So much had been said about the crossing, Lorenzo concluded, that the sailors had merely exaggerated the dangers to play up the fear.

But as they approached the strait, all of the men, even those who had been asleep, were awake and anxious on deck. *The threats here must lurk below the surface*, Lorenzo thought, *not visible to the untrained crewman.* The *San Lorenzo* sailed out without incident until she approached the island of Biri. Don Alfonso maneuvered the ship in a zigzag path until it cleared one of the two major rock formations that formed an underwater obstacle course. Hitting any one of those dangerous obstacles could mean the sinking of the ship and perhaps the loss of many lives.

Slowly, they navigated through their chief fears. The crew did everything they could to avoid running aground on the coastline, clipping the ship on the rock formations, or even worse, slamming onto them full force. Sails were lowered and the Filipino crew propped themselves on the dinghy, a small boat that would tow the giant galleon into open ocean. Sweeping as hard as they could with the oars, they made headway with the receding tide, which they had to clear before the waters became too shallow. The rumble of the waves did nothing to alleviate the tension, because the experienced sailors knew the sea was not always what it seemed. Though the passage could prove swift, their concerns remained because the wind, which was blowing against them, barred a full advance into the open ocean.

Blowing in from the southeast and heading in their direction was a flock of birds, one of the first signs of an impending storm. The ship's captain and ship's master debated the possibility of turning back, since they were still close to shore and could anchor at Biri's final *embarcadero*. But the tides were too low and a decision to turn back could risk damaging the ship's hull. The best they could do was ride out the storm on the open sea.[1]

"Full speed ahead," Don Jorge ordered the pilot. "And get those sails up, Officer Carlos." Their goal was to face the oncoming storm as far into sea—and as far from the dangers of the strait—as possible. "Raise the sails!" With whatever airstream they could ride and all possible maneuverings of the galleon, the ship and all the people on board advanced at a swift and steady eight knots.

As chaplain, Father Antonio intoned a prayer for safety. He was joined by the ship's pages as well as the other priests: "Our Lady of Good Voyage, patroness of safe journeys, spread the mantel of your maternal protection over us throughout this journey. Through your intercession and loving guidance, may our ship arrive intact at our earthly destination. And when our lives are over, please stand on the shore and lead us into the eternal embrace of your Divine Son. Amen. Lord, God almighty, have mercy on us poor sinners."

The priests then heard a succession of confessions from the officers and crew. Enduring the storm would be bad enough. But the storm could prove deadly, and if they didn't survive it—and had not adequately prepared their souls—that would be even worse.

"Ease the sails!" Don Jorge roared, after they were a considerable distance from land. "Ease the sails!" echoed Don Carlos, the boatswain. The apprentices worked frantically at the riggings and scaled the masts, readying the yards for any onslaught of stormy weather.

A relay of orders sounded down the length of the ship from the stern deck to prow.

"Lower the anchors," yelled the captain. "Lower the anchors," boomed the ship's master.

"Lower the anchors, you miserable peons," repeated the boatswain, supplementing the order with his own address to the crew.

In anticipation of the storm and its aftermath, Giuseppe and Lorenzo prepared two days' worth of meals for the officers and crew. They would be battling not only wind and rain but also incessant noise, and the dangerous sway of advancing typhoon wind gusts that could easily push the ship, and even tip it over.

The crew secured all cargo below decks and then gathered and moved the live animals down to the first deck. The pigs squealed frantically as two sailors carried them below with their legs tied around a yoke. A rooster crowed as young hens clucked nervously, their heads with red combs and wattles jerking back and forth like warning devices.

Bulky and ominous clouds threatened overhead,

moving in above the seascape. But the sun's rays still fanned glowingly behind, outlining them in a thin rim of silver. Then everything died down to a standstill.

It was calm for six hours; then the storm unleashed its power. The *San Lorenzo* was pelted with rain, a seemingly pathetic warning of the total damage to come. A whirring sound coiled about them. It was the wind, and with it, waves that descended into troughs as deep as valleys and ascended the crests as high as mountains. The ship rocked dangerously.

It was becoming more difficult to hear any of the orders being barked on deck. The noise, like a grinding millstone, cancelled out any intelligible sound. The full force of the typhoon had finally arrived, and whipped yards of sail to shreds. Lorenzo saw how the men knew exactly what to do; with next to no sailing experience himself, all Lorenzo knew how to do was take cover. Rain swept across them in heavy bands that wiped away any chance of clear vision.

Below, the Filipino sailors were gearing up for working the pumps after seawater had washed profusely on deck and flooded into the hold. They began working the levers of the bilge pumps even as the storm advanced overhead. When waves finally crashed on deck, the crew's efforts grew more futile, but ever more necessary. The men held on to the levers for dear life, as the ship's rocking threw them about.

Lorenzo carefully made his way down into the hold to the first deck, where a faint light glowing in a lantern revealed the terrified faces of three pages. A line was drawn on the side of the ship to mark the safe level for water to rise. If the water level breached this mark, it meant likely death unless the captain ordered the crew to abandon ship and they somehow managed to survive at sea until they washed ashore. The battle was for the present moment. Their only weapons were the pumps. But nature held the upper hand.

It was not uncommon for stormy seas to break through a ship's hull, and the painful creaking of the ship alerted them to a new level of anxiety. Food rations would spoil from water damage, so there would be little to consume after the storm passed. They still had at least a few days more at sea before they reached Formosa. That was, if the storm did not blow them off course directly toward Japan instead.

The pages guided Lorenzo up to the second deck with them. They were only as old as Lorenzo's two young sons. *At least my boys aren't in a place like this,* he thought. *How frightened they would be!* To Lorenzo, the howling sound of the wind was the worst part of all. It was as if some unseen thing had come hunting for its prey, spooking the men out of their hiding places to make the final kill. "O Lord, how long will you keep your protective hand from us? Guide us, Lord, guide us to safety," Lorenzo prayed quietly.

For a day he and the pages stayed in the hold of the second deck, sickened with fear. The pages munched on small cubes of cheese and salt meat like little mice. Water was everywhere, streaming down the sides of the ship and collecting into the bilge. But the pumping continued above because the water level had not yet breached the danger line.

On what he reckoned was the second day, Lorenzo made a concentrated effort to get back up onto the main deck. He held on tightly to the sides of the ladder, sometimes pushing his back against the side of the boat to keep steady on his feet. At the surface, the sky was a muddled gray. A number of the crew was still at the bilge pump working the lever; some looked ready to collapse. Discovering that some of them had not been relieved of this duty since the storm began, Lorenzo joined in the effort.

Lorenzo tried to wrench Guapo from his post so that the man could get something to eat in the hold, but Guapo seemed to refuse to let go. Lorenzo found that the man had been attached to the lever by a rope tied around his wrists. Whoever had done this had made sure that Guapo and the others could not escape. But the ropes had also prevented them from being swept into the turbulent sea.

Lorenzo made his way below deck, stuffed his pocket with small bits of food, and returned to feed the Filipino lever operators by hand. They had survived the ordeal only by catching the rainfall in their mouths.

When the storm began to abate, the friars, along with the barber who also served as the ship's surgeon, laid the injured crewmen on the second deck bunk areas and sorted them out according to the seriousness of their injuries. Injuries included fingers crushed by shifting cargo, various gashes and wounds from falling masts and rigging, and innumerable splinters in their faces—one even in an eye, already swollen with infection. The eye would have to be removed, or it was likely the sailor would not survive. Giuseppe managed to get some water boiling on the stove. Some of the crew held the poor man down while the barber plucked out the infected eye and cauterized the cavity with a glowing iron rod. The wailing was infernal.

Much of the crew simply lay down on the sodden main deck, passed out from extreme exhaustion. Lorenzo noticed that the bilge levers had finally stopped pumping water. Its five remaining Filipino workers were slumped down against it motionless. It was not until a couple of hours had passed that he realized they were dead. Guapo was counted among them.

The boatswain was swift in his duty. He cut the tethers from the dead men's wrists and ordered that they be wrapped in separate shrouds made from shreds of damaged sail. The gunner and navy officer delivered exactly five cannonballs to where the deceased had been laid. They inserted them under their feet, to weigh the bodies down in the water. But before they were tossed unceremoniously overboard, Lorenzo begged that prayers be said for their souls. Lazaro, the leper from Kyoto, escorted Father Vicente up to the main deck for this last act of mercy. He conducted swift but earnest prayers for all five, asking another Filipino crewman for the full names of the deceased, which he promptly listed in his Bible.

After Father Vicente concluded the ceremony with a blessing, Lorenzo, Giuseppe, and Manuel, the Portuguese caulker, slid the bodies down a plank and into the watery grave. In half an hour it was over.

It seemed almost surreal when the sun broke through the clouds and opened a portal of light upon the galleon. Throughout the afternoon and through the next few days, the crew was busy repairing the ship. Lorenzo and Giuseppe salvaged what they could of the food supplies and prepared meals for the able-bodied, as well as the sick and recuperating crewmembers. New sails were created from yardage of canvas unbolted on the main deck. Hemp fiber from Philippine copra plants had proven to be the best material for ropes because they had not frayed much even with constant friction.

It was during compline, the last prayers of the day, that Lorenzo could offer a worthy personal prayer for those who had suffered most in the storm. Lorenzo prayed especially for Guapo, with his ulcerated face and insulting nickname, and his four friends. They had saved the entire ship, because they kept it from sinking while working the pumps on deck for two straight days.

Lorenzo read aloud from the Book of Job. The words expressed Job's unrestrained bewilderment at the Lord's ways, and contempt for his own life. His own feelings were not so far removed from such grief.

[He] who alone stretched out the heavens and
  trampled the waves of the Sea;
who made the Bear and Orion, the Pleiades and the
  chambers of the south;
who does great things beyond understanding, and
  marvelous things without number.
Look, he passes by me, and I do not see him; he
  moves on, but I do not perceive him.
He snatches away; who can stop him? Who will say
  to him, "What are you doing?"[2]

# Formosa

# CHAPTER 7

"*Ay*, Lorenzo," murmured Father Miguel—putting a reassuring hand on Lorenzo's shoulder. The priest's demeanor seemed unaltered by the recent tragedy at sea, as terrible as it had been for everyone. Father Miguel considered Lorenzo a peer because they were about the same age. He noticed, too, as had the others in their missionary expedition, that Lorenzo had withdrawn further into himself. "Under the weight of grief, the heart suffers and yearns for company," he continued. "Lorenzo, if you only knew what it took to get us to this point. It isn't very far from your home, I know, but it is farther than we could have gone otherwise without some divine guidance."

"*Sí, sí, Padre. Yo entiendo*," Lorenzo nodded absently—looking out onto the borderless horizon. "I do not mean to be ungrateful. But I understand only what I've been told in bits and pieces," he added as an afterthought. "This is the farthest I've ever gone in my whole life," Lorenzo said. "Being away from family and home . . . it's a pitiable state all around, Father."

"Yes, absolutely," Father Miguel said, mindful of the separations and sacrifices he himself had made. "But haven't we become your family, too, Lorenzo? Please believe we are," he begged. "Do you know how difficult it was for our provincial superior, Father Domingo Gonzales, to sneak us out of Manila?"

Lorenzo snapped to attention at the mention of Father Domingo's name. He transfixed his gaze on the priest. Lorenzo had known Father Domingo since he had served as an altar boy for Masses at the Santo Domingo Convent in Intramuros, the walled city of Manila. It was to him that Father Antonio had sent Lorenzo when he needed advice on how to deal sensibly with the Guardia Civil. An anxious time it was then, but Lorenzo could only guess at what Father Miguel was hinting.

"*Por favor, Padre.* I am a willing listener. Please tell me."

"You may or may not know this, Lorenzo," said Father Miguel while darting a nervous glance at those within earshot. "But this was our third attempt to leave," he whispered. "The government of Japan had put an official ban on missionaries arriving from Manila."

"*Sí, sí,* I know," said Lorenzo.

"It made Japan into a 'forbidden land' for us priests. And our current Governor-General . . ." he continued, whispering. "Sebastian Hurtado de Corcuera was watching us closely, very closely. Corcuera would enforce the ban on us leaving for Japan."

"This I do know, Father. He also believed that Father Domingo . . ."

" . . . our Dominican superior,"

" . . . was up to something," Lorenzo interrupted.

"True. Would you like to switch places and tell me the rest of the story, Lorenzo?" Father Miguel said in good humor.

"Pardon me, Father. I only know so much," Lorenzo gestured rather deferentially, his thin grin hidden behind a small pinch of his forefinger and thumb.

"All right," Father Miguel continued. "Well, as I was saying, this was our third attempt to leave Manila for Japan. And, I must say, it was bold and courageous on Father Antonio's part to move ahead with the plans, especially after we found out that the Governor-General himself was in Cavite at the time of our departure."

Lorenzo's eyes broadened with surprise and confusion.

"Corcuera? He was . . . ? And how could he miss what was going on right under his nose, Padre? You made no attempt to even conceal or change your priestly clothing?"

"Indeed," Father Miguel answered. "And do you know that Corcuera has set up numerous checkpoints along the route from Manila to Cavite, even sending out a ship into Manila Bay to intercept Chinese sampans and Malayan *praos* that might have passengers even remotely like us aboard them? That helped us, you see. Our first two attempts failed because we planned our escape aboard a sampan. That's what they were expecting all along. But no one dared to imagine anything as remotely absurd as what we actually accomplished—boarding one of the galleons."

"Oh, good Lord. It was bold."

"Yes, that was what Father Antonio said. He reasoned that the more brazen the attempt, the less likely we were to get caught."

"Was it worth the risk for you?" Lorenzo asked. "I mean, what if you were to get caught? And I, too, could have gotten caught . . . ?" Lorenzo added, knowing that the consequences would have been unthinkable for himself and his family. Seeing that he felt a little weak in the knees, Father

Miguel looked at Lorenzo directly, and nodded slowly. "And what of the captain, Don Enrique? Hasn't he put himself and his ship in jeopardy as well?"

"Not only Don Enrique, but the two other captains in our convoy as well. They were also in on our little plot."

"Why? How?" The risk of staying in Manila far outweighed those of escape, Lorenzo knew, especially for him. But still, he wondered if he had been better off not knowing about all the intrigue, and the number of people who had taken chances that had benefitted him.

"It's a play of many things, Lorenzo—friendship, a sense of fairness, indebtedness, vision, mission, a Dominican connection—all the things God stirs into our lives that makes some things happen and others not. It was God's ordaining will, he *wants* it to happen; or it was his permitting will, he *allows* it to occur. But it is always to accomplish some greater good in the end. God respects our free will, our decisions to yield to his will or not. We are on God's mission to help the persecuted faithful in Japan, Lorenzo. They wrote to us in desperate need of the sacraments and the care of a pastor. Was it worth the risk? I say, 'Yes,' even for the benefit of one soul, it is. Still, as you already know, none of us are 'on record' as passengers aboard this ship. And it will be some time before we discover what awaits us in Okinawa."

"Okinawa . . ." Lorenzo's journey was to end in Formosa. "Was it not an independent kingdom for some time, Father?"

"Yes, but about thirty years ago a Japanese clan from Satsuma took hold of it so that they could get a piece of the China trade which had been restricted in mainland Japan. Word has reached us that Catholic missionaries who have made it to Okinawa are not—how should I say it?—not always fortunate either."

"Why? What happened to them?"

"Missionaries have been arrested and killed. Arrested and killed," Father Miguel repeated. "So, we don't know what awaits us in Japan. Nevertheless, we must maintain our faith, Lorenzo—we trust that no matter what happens to us, God will always be there to provide what we need at every moment."

The two men stood silent, each lost in a moment of sobering thought.

"How, exactly, do you intend to reach Okinawa from Formosa?" Lorenzo asked, breaking the pause.

"That is where we'll change into regular clothes."

"Like Spanish gentlemen, I am sure."

"Just plain foreigners, Lorenzo, to match our faces. That's what we'll be and appear to be to others wherever we are in Asia. You, of course will not need to do this. Because of your Chinese heritage you will blend right in." But Lorenzo could not see what made him any different. Anywhere outside the Philippines was as foreign to him as it was to them.

"You will look like traders," Lorenzo said.

"Yes, I suppose. Perhaps, in a way, we are."

"I shall plan to stay in Formosa," Lorenzo said more in reassurance than determination. "I may try to make my way to Macao afterward, once I have started a new life and I can send for my family."

"Well, our choice seems to be much simpler than yours," Father Miguel replied, to which they shared a nervous laugh.

"Whatever God wills, let it be," Lorenzo said, his heart somewhere between struggle and resignation.

"You can always join us," Father Miguel suggested.

"We'll see, Father. You might not have much use for a scribe in Japan. But my wife and children need me very much."

"Everyone needs a good person, Lorenzo."

"Thank you, Father. Anyway, who knows? You all might be denied entry into Okinawa, and find yourselves back in Manila. And I'll be there all alone in Formosa. You will send word to my wife, won't you? You'll let R-R-Rosario know about me, Father?" Her name caught in his throat.

"Yes, of course, Lorenzo. I'm sure we can manage that, no matter what."

Lorenzo knew he was a last-minute addition to the friars' mission. The friars knew he needed to escape Manila immediately and they chose to help him. He had faced either execution or slave labor that some members of the Guardia Civil had proposed for him aboard a galleon. *The irony of it all,* Lorenzo thought to himself, as he worked the galley. He had incurred the resentment and envy of some members of the Guardia Civil, perhaps because he enjoyed a rare status for an *Indio*. The paradox of escape and bonded service lay in the reality of his present circumstances. He had accepted free passage and evaded the possible forced servitude only to render it willingly aboard the *San Lorenzo*. *But there is merit in this sacrifice,* he thought. Here, he had experienced firsthand the perennial hardships of the other *Indios* aboard ship. In a way everything since he had left home had turned into a genuine penance, one Lorenzo had embraced unwillingly at first and even grudgingly for now. But for the meantime he had opened himself up to the possibilities that lay ahead. *What else is there for me to lose? Time, or something more?*

∽

The men on the second deck engaged in some onboard amusements such as cards and dice. And although gambling was strictly forbidden, the men often placed bets while playing. Don Carlos turned a blind eye to what was happening. As a seasoned seaman, Don Carlos knew that this bit of diversion could help them relax a bit after the turmoil they had undergone at sea.

The ship's Spanish notary, or *escríbano*, had joined the game as well this afternoon and was raking in some tidy winnings. It would have gone unnoticed above deck if a quarrel had not broken out.

"You don't seem to be a very good guardian of your money!" the *escríbano* shouted to Gabriel, the ship's *guardiane*. "You one-eyed jackal!" retorted an angry Gabriel, who then rammed his fist into the *escríbano*'s good eye. The ruckus could easily be heard above. Don Enrique quickly descended and promptly ended the melée, but not without first confiscating the *escríbano*'s loot and placing it in Father Antonio's pocket. "Consider it a donation, Father Antonio," said Don Enrique emphatically. Recalling how the Dominicans had been forced to pay more when they first boarded, both men recognized the irony in it. Only Father Antonio, however, was laughing. The *escríbano* did not take his sudden loss well, and approached the cleric with a threat of vengeance.

"I *will* get that back, Padre," he said through gritted teeth. "I'll get my money and interest, I promise you."

Don Enrique dismissed his *escríbano*'s remarks and ordered him to apologize. "You will set matters straight before this voyage is over, *escríbano*, and give to God's messengers what is justly due. That is what's best for your soul," he said.

The *escríbano* replied with an overly exaggerated gentleman's bow toward Father Antonio. "I will yield for now, *Señor*. But gains of this sort can bring with them a certain curse, wouldn't you say so, Padre?"

"What we yield freely to God, he gives tenfold back to the giver, *escríbano*. God will not be outdone in generosity, my son," said Father Antonio. "There are those who will benefit from this small fortune. And our prayers go with you, who share it with us."

"Very well, prayers all around to sanctify the sinner, Padre," the *escríbano* sneered. "You and I will certainly be in need of them."

"Perhaps you should join the others up on deck," advised Father Antonio. "The fresh air will do you good. They are listening to Don Carlos reading to them. You will not be disappointed."

"What exactly is the boatswain reading now to those pitiful dogs, I wonder?"

"Dante's 'Inferno.'"

"Very amusing, Padre. I could write a few verses about hell myself."

All of a sudden one of the apprentices, atop his perch on the mainmast, gave the cry they had all been waiting for, "¡*Veo la tierra*! I see land!"

With that, everything that had been transpiring abruptly ended, and all able bodies ascended the ladder to the main deck. The sun was at a good angle in the sky; it was just a little before noon.

"Has the voyage worn you out, Padre? It's only been three weeks," teased Don Enrique. "For us, this is a mere stopover. Wait till you resume your voyage across the Pacific. *Then* you will be able to say that you have really sailed. But for now we must prepare for arrival. God be with you, *mi amigo*."

"May he be with you, too, *hijo*." Their holy collaboration ended with a mere grasp of the shoulders.

Within a short while the galleon was tied at port. Without delay, Giuseppe and the others hopped off the *San Lorenzo* after terse nods and disappeared into the sea of humanity on the pier. *There is even more commotion arriving than there was at departure,* thought Lorenzo. Something about making their destination triggered an almost giddy joy among the crew. But here, in Formosa, was where Lorenzo would disembark and go his separate way from the friars' missionary expedition to Japan. So much had happened in the last three weeks that it seemed like a lifetime ago since he had seen his family. In the moment, he had almost forgotten that he would not be seeing the friendly and brave Dominicans much longer.

It took the rest of the day to disembark, and then it took several hours more for those who had made the trip to maintain firm footing on actual ground. For injured sailors, the ship's arrival in port meant their voyage was over. They would receive no further pay. The bustle leaving the *San Lorenzo* was almost matched by the traffic approaching it. Arrivals in port meant fresh customers for almost every kind of business. Seasoned pier vendors were among the first to come up to the passengers, offering tempting layered cakes of Portuguese *bebinca,* a kind of baked pudding.

Before leaving the vessel, the Dominicans changed into clothes of a clearly cultivated Iberian style, effectively hiding their true priestly identity. Lorenzo thought some of what they wore might have been borrowed from the captain and the ship's master. What he particularly admired were their high-cut leather boots. In a show of respect for Lorenzo, all of them removed their hats, save for Father Guillermo, the light-haired Frenchman, who had no head covering at all. The Japanese priest, Father Vicente, had simply changed into a full-length black kimono with a second covering on top of it—a kind of coat called *haori.* Lazaro of Kyoto, the leper, wore similar attire, but his *kimono* had a hood to conceal the facial disfigurements that were the hallmarks of his wasting disease.

From Formosa, the missionaries had already made arrangements to secure passage to Japan via a Chinese *sampan*. This was where they and Lorenzo would part ways. "Are you ready for all this?" Father Antonio motioned to Lorenzo as the disguised friars and Lazaro headed up the pier with their belongings.

"Yes, I suppose so," Lorenzo replied.

They seemed to be an odd grouping of men among the Chinese in Formosa, clearly foreign, but not unlike the other travelers in their midst. Still, there was something noble about the way they walked and a certain modesty in their expressions. *Perhaps they are saying vespers to themselves,* Lorenzo conjectured. Whatever it was, clothing could not be used to conceal that these men were priests, he thought to himself. *They give themselves away by their gait.*

"Again, we welcome your company, Lorenzo, should you opt to join us to Japan," Father Antonio repeated.

The persistence of the invitation disturbed Lorenzo. It was as if the good friars knew something that he did not. Looking for an answer, Lorenzo recalled Father Miguel's words: *The Lord always respects free will.*

"What determines our fate, Father?"

"Fate is not 'determined' at all, Lorenzo. You . . . I . . . we are all given free will to make our own decisions. God, who is eternal, already knows what decisions we've made and will make. But in any case, we choose within the spheres that we find ourselves. Sometimes our circumstances are of our own making; at other times they are imposed upon us. Remember that nothing ever goes to waste with God. He loves us in complete mercy. We are the ones who condemn ourselves to eternal damnation. How we act and what motivates us to act in such a way, our intentions—God always sees everything. In the end, he will judge us by our hearts, by how much and how well we have loved."

"If I stay, what does that imply, I wonder?"

"It means you want to stay," Father Antonio teased.

"And if I go with you . . ."

"It means you appreciate our company." A long pause came after the brief laughter. "Regardless of what you decide, know that we will respect your decision. And surely, we will all miss you, son."

Lorenzo took Father Antonio's hand and placed it respectfully to his own forehead in a Filipino gesture reserved for elders in appeal for their blessings.

"God be with you," Father Antonio said.

"And with you, Father." Lorenzo watched as Father Antonio made his way up the dock to join the rest. A sense of bitter isolation and deep loneliness engulfed Lorenzo immediately.

# CHAPTER 8

"I'd be a fool to leave Formosa simply because of all this dripping sentiment," Lorenzo said to himself. "I have already lost my wife and children. What is one more farewell?" It was not long after he had turned away in the other direction and wiped his eyes clean, however, that Lorenzo was unexpectedly confronted by the ship's *escríbano*.

Lurking like a serpent on the pier, he had been loitering close to the galleon, and had observed Lorenzo's entire conversation with Father Antonio.

"*Indio*," he hissed. "Where are you going?"

Lorenzo ignored him. It was clear the *escríbano* had already wasted part of his earnings on liquor and was drunk.

"Hey, *Indio*," he called out again, this time with more bile. "I know why you are here."

Lorenzo hurried his pace and darted between shanties for brief cover. But the vindictive *escríbano* was intent on evening the score and pursued him.

"Yes, I know what you are, Lorenzo. A murderer, a murderer indeed. An assassin!" he cried out in venomous anger. "That is what you are—a wanted man, Lorenzo. I know this. And I bet all my earnings that you will be caught, right here in Formosa. *¡Usted es un criminal!*"

Lorenzo could have ignored the shouts of a drunken sailor. But it appeared that people had heard the *escríbano's* rants, and had stopped to watch what would happen next. Lorenzo knew it would not take much for the Chinese on Formosa to distrust him. As the *escríbano* moved on, Lorenzo started to feel shaky and sat down to compose himself. It appeared that he still had sea legs and had forgotten how to walk on solid ground.

After an hour or so, he ventured to purchase a small meal of rice and fish from a pier vendor. But not one of them would take his money. Someone motioned for him to go away. Another spat at his feet. *Had the escribano's words already caused people to blacklist him,* Lorenzo wondered.

But perhaps the biggest threat was what he thought he saw back at the wharf. It looked to him as if the Spanish *escríbano* handed something to a couple of Spanish guards. Lorenzo wondered if his mind was playing tricks on him, if he was being overly suspicious, or if somehow Formosa had become as dangerous for him as it seemed.

In the midst of this internal confusion, a Chinese-Filipina woman approached him. She seemed more curious than sympathetic to his plight. But after a moment, she revealed that her Chinese husband worked as a casual trader on the pier, and told Lorenzo the exchange she had overheard between the *escríbano* and the Spanish civil guards when she was returning from visiting her husband. It was not at all what Lorenzo might have expected or imagined.

With a mind for profit, the woman said, the *escríbano* had negotiated an exchange of paid information for the arrest of a Father Antonio and whoever his companions were. She feared that Lorenzo, because he had been mentioned along with the priests, might also be at risk.

"Human greed stops at nothing," she said. "You had

better get word to your friends, because there will be no delay in arresting them."

Though Lorenzo felt indebted to the woman for alerting him, he also feared inadvertently leading the Spanish authorities and spies on the pier—who were seemingly following him—to the Dominicans, if they had not yet sailed for Japan. But curiosity took the better of him for the moment.

"Why did you come to help me?" he asked.

"It just seemed like you needed help and it cost me nothing to provide it."

"How did you know that I was a *kababayan*, a fellow Filipino?"

"I didn't," she said plainly. "Imagine that," she added, smiling as if his honesty were itself her reward.

Lorenzo pulled something from out of his belongings and handed it to her in gratitude before disappearing into the maze of small buildings and winding paths. She opened her hand to find a rosary of wooden beads. Putting it to her lips, she kissed it. Perhaps they had had something even deeper in common.

It was in the unholy hours of early morning prayers when Lorenzo eventually chanced upon a sampan on a far section of the wharf. He had already made a random search of many of the boats at the dock. In fact the vessel before him seemed to be under repair. *If the Spanish civil guards had been serious about making an arrest, they would have certainly beaten me to this place,* he thought. It was Father Guillermo's light hair reflecting off the internal glow of the cabin that signaled success for Lorenzo. He knew he had found his Dominican brothers.

"Ahoy there, inside," he began with care. Someone cautiously put out the flame of the lantern.

"Who goes there?" another man asked in the Fukien Chinese dialect.

"Tell the good friars it is Lorenzo," he responded quietly. Father Miguel alighted nimbly from the sampan and took Lorenzo by the arm, leading him into the boat.

"Something happened, and I have changed my mind," Lorenzo said with the relief of knowing he would not be alone. "But I also have some troubling news. We are all at risk." With that the Dominicans evacuated the sampan and moved swiftly across the shore to an even more remote pier used only by the locals. They returned to the boat just before dawn, and by first light set sail with the wind, heading northeast to the territories of the Ryukyu monarchs and the island of Okinawa.

By midmorning their Chinese ship's pilot had made it to the closest outer reaches of the Yaeyama Islands, one of three major divisions in the Kingdom of Okinawa. The Ryukyu ruled a string of more than 100 tiny islands that reached from the southwest end of Japan to Formosa. Less than half of them were inhabited.

With their Chinese sampan coursing rather listlessly through the waters, the rays of the rising sun challenged their vision to the east in a crimson fan of light. The pilot had set out as a matter of recourse into the deep. And because the fishing season had not yet begun in earnest, he and the Dominicans had little concern about receiving unwelcome attention.

The men each kept their silence. Unlike the big galleon on which they had been for three weeks the sampan sailed low on the waters, giving them a view of nature they could not have seen before. They could see coral gleaming beneath the crystal-clear waters. Blue lagoons merged into shallow aqua pools, and reached as far out as they could see. The sun had just barely lifted above the horizon when the Chinese guide asked his son Lee to collapse the sampan sail. "Dear reverends," he announced, "we shall stay here awhile and try our luck at catching breakfast."

The Dominicans were roused from their quiet contemplation and agreed that with the bounty of the sea all around them, there could be no better opportunity to chance upon a meal.

But Lorenzo stood purposefully at the edge of the sampan, with one foot on the rim of the boat. Then without further hesitation, he stripped down to his underwear and jumped artlessly into the water for a swim. The salt water quickly made his eyes sting, but nothing could have felt more wonderful.

The friars laughed at this burst of spontaneity and without much encouragement, followed suit. One after another they undressed, and threw themselves into the water. After three weeks at sea and a single overnight stay on land, not one of them had yet bathed since leaving Manila. Lice had powdered their hair with rabid infestation and Lorenzo's clothes, at least, seemed more than ready to be shed like dead skin. Only Lazaro of Kyoto remained onboard.

The two fishermen indulged the clerics and their assistant for half an hour while they readied their fishing lines. Then the older fisherman advised the men to return aboard the sampan. "A tuna," he cautioned, "will most assuredly drag the boat a good distance."

Timing the casting of their line with the movement of a school of fish, the fishermen hooked onto a large catch without much of a wait. The bonito fish were hungry themselves and competed for the bait. But it was the tuna the fishermen were angling for. In fine form, the huge tuna they soon caught put up a gallant fight and towed the boat some distance on the open waters before it weakened into thrashing about. Fearing the loss of their catch, the men took turns pulling it slowly toward the sampan. This tug-of-war lasted for a good two hours, with periods of easing the line before the fishermen finally reeled the embattled tuna into the boat. Even with its bulging eyes, it was a large, handsome fish—three to five years old, and a good six feet long,

Though he was shorter than their catch, the Chinese fisherman bashed the tuna's head to knock it semiconscious, and thrust his knife into the fish's belly.

And while it instinctively wriggled and thrashed, the fisherman disemboweled the fish clean. Copious amounts of blood spilled into the boat, coating the bottom with a vibrant red that rose above the men's ankles. Lee, the fisherman's son, did his best to wash the fish—and the sampan—with sea-water. Reflexive movement caused the tuna to gasp, but there was nothing with which to hold the air in its cavity. The fishermen knew better than to throw anything overboard until they were ready to commence sailing. This low to the water the entrails would become an enticing slurry for sharks. In the meantime they were all steeped in a bloody red stew of raw fish innards that included the half-digested remains of squid and mackerel.

They searched for anything of modest height aboard the sampan and stood on it. Then with the ceremony and care of a trained swordsman, the elder fisherman handled chunks of meat and sliced them thinly on a clean board, washed the pieces in brine, and lightly cooked them in Chinese vinegar.

Father Vicente and Lazaro of Kyoto eagerly consumed their fish, which was served in the Japanese manner. With balls of hot rice cooked in a clay pot that rested above its clay stove, their meal came as a rare treat. It took a bit of coaxing before the Spanish friars surrendered to their hunger and in modest portions discovered that the tuna tasted unlike anything they had ever eaten before. It was not consumed, however, without a blessing first and the requisite grace before meals. Father Antonio recalled what Tertullian, an early Church father, had written about the fish as a symbol of Christian faith and Baptism. "We, little fishes, after the image of our Jesus Christ, are born in the water, nor have we safety in any other way than by permanently abiding in this water."

Sailing on the East China Sea past the Miyako islands, where they had eaten breakfast, the sampan found its bearings and headed northeast to the large island of Okinawa. While en route the men devoutly prayed the Rosary. The friars considered it a spiritual pilgrimage, feeling the beads running through their hands and the prayers passing through their lips; even their thoughts and memories led them to places beyond the sampan. In meditation they made mystical journeys through the life of Christ: joyfully in Nazareth and Bethlehem, sorrowfully in Jerusalem, and gloriously to heaven, where Mary, the Mother of God, reigned as queen.

For Lorenzo, the Rosary was also a spiritual journey. Through it, he could feel the love that connected him to his wife and children. In that love, Lorenzo commended his family to the care of the Holy Family, reflecting on the simple and hidden life shared by Jesus, Mary, and Joseph—one not so different from the life he had left behind.

The weeklong sail seemed relatively short. By the evening of July 10, they had arrived and hastily proceeded under the cover of darkness to a secluded cove on the Okinawan coast. Though it had come under the widening influence of Japan's power, Okinawa was a small, independent kingdom, historically ruled by the Ryukyu dynasty. Hoping to come across some secret Christians, Father Antonio sighed with exhaustion as they walked, "No, God will not deny us a welcoming household."

Summer had reached its peak in Okinawa, and the

pungent smell of the earth rose from beneath their footsteps. Their arrival had coincided with the typhoon season and the Chinese fishermen were keen to return to Formosa before heavy rains postponed their return.

"We shall moor here, Fathers," the older fisherman said to the Dominican friars. He raised three fingers indicating how many nights' stay they would make before heading back home. "If we do not receive word from you within this time, we will assume that you are all right. May we agree on this, Father?"

Father Antonio nodded and gave them a blessing. "Please, dispose of our belongings," he instructed of their priestly garb. "Bury them in the mountains, when you get a chance or tear them into rags for your use."

"Good Father, thank you for all you have done for us. Please, it is your presence that has brought blessings for this fishing vessel."

"Hush now, my son. God be with you and your son. You owe us nothing. It is because of you that we have come this far. Pray for us, that our time here will be fruitful according to God's will."

# CHAPTER 9

The men found their way to the outskirts of Naha, to accommodations in what seemed a rather informal inn somewhere in a lightly traveled part of town, where few, if any, foreigners were staying. Most preferred to lodge in the main city of Naha, some eighteen miles away. At the inn, a Ryukyuan woman dressed in a plain-dyed outfit, similar to a kimono, met them at the base of the steps. She assisted each one with hospitable efficiency, drawing for each of them a warm bath in a wooden shed toward the rear of the house. Quickly aware of Lazaro of Kyoto's condition, she directed him to a nearby stream.

After they had eaten, the friars and Lorenzo fell soundly asleep, each in their private quarters. Lorenzo was assigned a smaller room by comparison, perhaps because it was apparent that he was a servant to the others. But only Lazaro of Kyoto was required to lodge outside of the inn because of his condition. It was their first real rest on land in a month.

The next morning the same woman served them breakfast. Father Antonio, through Lazaro's assistance as a translator, attempted to pay for two days more in advance.

But the innkeeper flatly refused any such arrangement. She merely charged them for their overnight board and lodging and asked that they settle their bills with her daily. Father Antonio hoped to scout around for any Christians who might be in the area, or at least anyone not hostile to Christians who would be willing to transport them without delay north to Japan. He knew that this would not be easily arranged, as there was a strict ban on foreigners in Japan. The Dominicans even considered the possibility of traveling in two separate groups—with the Japanese contingent making their way more easily into their territory and the European delegation with Lorenzo following covertly by some other means. Father Antonio decided against it, however, because he believed their security and effectiveness depended on their staying together as one group.

Father Antonio then assigned Father Vicente to search for Christians and make travel arrangements with locals he discerned to be trustworthy. Lorenzo would accompany him on this day mission, moving about easily in the outskirts of Naha, while Lazaro of Kyoto would remain with the friars as translator for them at the inn. The three European friars retired to silent contemplation and continual prayer for their mission's success. They instructed the innkeeper that they would not be partaking of any lunch. As gaunt as they had become from their voyage, they offered the fast as a small sacrifice for their mission.

At midday the innkeeper politely knocked on the door to Father Antonio's room and asked if he and the rest of the men would enjoy some entertainment or female company for the night. They politely refused her invitation, making the excuse that they were still quite exhausted and needed more rest to regain their strength.

In the afternoon of that same day, however, the Dominicans began to sense that something was wrong, when the innkeeper returned again to suggest female companionship, which they flatly refused once more. They found her persistence to be troubling but the Dominicans were careful to dismiss the woman kindly, for they knew it was difficult to find other lodgings in the area without drawing suspicion to themselves. They assumed that their hostess didn't know that they were Christian clerics, and for their personal protection it was essential that they keep this fact hidden.

Many moneyed traders from China, Japan, and other Asian countries landed in Naha to engage in business and commerce, as well as to indulge their sinful desires in the pleasure district. But this was not a brothel, at least not to their knowledge.

They conducted themselves calmly, remaining mostly silent the rest of the day while they waited for Father Vicente and Lorenzo to return from their travels on foot. Unfortunately, when the pair returned the news was rather disappointing. The mission had not been as successful as they had hoped. Lorenzo pointed out that they discovered that there seemed to have been a Catholic church in the area at one time, but it had been converted into an inn. Father Vicente asserted that there must be some remnants of a Catholic community in Naha, but suggested they continue the discussion in the morning after a good night's rest had given them a fresh perspective on their situation. They all agreed.

After a supper of rice and fish, they each retired to their quarters and again settled down to sleep on their mats. Father Antonio decided that it would be best if they departed for Naha before sunrise. He concluded that nothing could be more dangerous than staying in their present location. It was clear that the dynamics of their interactions with the innkeeper were becoming increasingly strained. So that night before going to bed he settled their bill with her.

Then something unexpected—and quite unwelcome—occurred. Without benefit of much light or the forewarning of sound, a woman slipped into Father Vicente's room in the middle of the night. Covered by little more than a veil, she lay down naked at his feet. Jolted from his light sleep by the movement she made, Father Vicente rose from his mat. As soon as he saw her he immediately threw his blanket over the woman to cover her defenselessness. In a whisper she offered her services to him as a prostitute.

The ploy startled the priest more for its desperation than for its crude attempt at seduction. He knew he had been lured into quite a predicament, and was fully aware that how he handled the situation could give away their reasons for coming to Okinawa. Celibacy was something that would appear suspicious to the Japanese. Careful of not giving himself away as a Catholic priest, Father Vicente firmly advised the young woman to don her kimono. She obeyed without hesitation.

"How old are you, my dear?" Father Vicente asked in a low, measured tone, trying to regain his composure.

"If it is my age that concerns you, there are other women . . ."

"No," Father Vicente replied, taking a deep breath. "That is not my worry."

Her name was Keiko. That much he learned. Initially, the kind friar spoke to her about matters more pertinent to self-preservation than to her welfare. But he remained curious at her refinement in the Japanese language and the fact that she held herself with such decorum that anyone could have mistaken her for a lady of the royal court. He learned that she was the daughter of a former samurai, who had lost his commission in Kyoto some years ago. In peacetime some of them had become warriors with no master or *ronin*. Keiko related how she had been somewhat coerced into her current lifestyle, because she could not endure the shame of her fallen station in Kyoto. She had stowed away to Okinawa, where she could remain fairly anonymous.

Father Vicente was surprised at her candor and sensed that the young woman's life was at a turning point. He could see that she was in need of both wise direction and genuine affection. Realizing that his response mattered more for the salvation of her soul than it did for his own, he encouraged her to leave her current profession and seek the goodness she wanted. Keiko seemed incredulous when he handed her what he had of his allowance of valued gold coins, change from the unproductive encounters he and Lorenzo had with the locals near Naha the previous day. She slipped away from his room well before sunrise, uplifted by the faithfulness and sincerity she had encountered.

In the morning Father Vicente mentioned the incident to the other friars and Lorenzo. Father Antonio was not surprised, but rather biting in his comments when he realized that the innkeeper had not sent *him* any temptations in the middle of the night. The others remarked that if it had happened, Father Antonio's likely outburst would have certainly had the townspeople descending on them all with swords and knives. Two of the other priests joked that any woman who came to their rooms would have had to abandon her trade for good because nothing but a real fire could rouse them from their slumber. Lorenzo listened to the priests' banter and was amazed at their outspokenness about such delicate matters. But he knew they were all men after all, and were doing their best to soothe Father Vicente, who remained flustered merely by describing the confrontation. Lorenzo's mind flashed to Rosario and his children back in Manila. *Deliver us from evil,* he prayed.

The Japanese priest seemed unable to let go of what had happened. But it was with poor Lazaro that Father Vicente pursued the matter in full. After some discussion, both men learned that by some working of Divine Providence, Lazaro of Kyoto might have been acquainted with the young woman's family. Lazaro shook his head with dismay and sadness at the degradation of similar young women in Japan—at how their circumstances led them to peddle dubious favors to gain material comfort, or more often just to survive. It was not as if these situations were unknown to either man. Yet, encountering it personally made the reality of trading in the flesh tangible. It was impossible not to be affected in some manner. The men offered solitary prayers for the young woman, asking God for her deliverance, and their strength against temptation.

Just before they left, the innkeeper sent word to the governor's office reporting the presence of these men at her inn. It was the accepted practice—one lifted from the entertainment courts in Ming China and the pleasure quarters of Edo and Kyoto in Japan—to alert authorities when patrons had stayed in the district for more than twenty-four hours. The Dominicans could not have known that their innkeeper had bound her establishment to such a convention.

Three days later, while the group trudged along the road to Naha, a contingent of Ryukyuan soldiers snared them. Despite struggling in order to evade capture, the Dominicans, Lazaro of Kyoto, and Lorenzo were ultimately taken into custody and arrested on suspicion of being Christians. What Lorenzo had feared most, had happened without much resistance on their part. And yet the gravity of what they were facing had not made its full impact on any of the accused.

They were escorted to the local jail just outside Naha. While there, the captives prayed and pondered what their next move would be. They were denied food for two days. Then, as they began to wonder if they would starve, Lorenzo, the Dominican friars, and Lazaro received help from an unexpected source . . . from someone they had not expected to see again. Keiko, the young prostitute, who, upon hearing what had become of the kind Father Vicente and his friends, took courage and made her way to where they were confined. She managed to curry favor with the guards so as to be able to smuggle food to the Dominicans and their companions. Over the days that followed, it was Keiko who cared for them in their need, developing a close rapport with Lazaro of Kyoto as well as with Father Vicente. His kindness had won Keiko over the night of their first meeting. During her visits to the local jail Father Vicente was able to speak to Keiko at length about Christ. It was there in the dreary cell that Keiko learned about the true Light of the World and then asked for and received the sacrament of Baptism at the hands of Father Vicente. The group's hope that their mission would at least be able to help one person was now fulfilled.

After Keiko's conversion the Dominicans were transferred to the dungeon in Shuri Castle, and Keiko escaped the Kingdom of Okinawa with the help of secret Christians. This hidden community of Christians had heard about the incarcerated clerics via a relay communication system, and in the same way as they had learned about the accused, they learned about Keiko. They were able to help her make her way to Portuguese Macao. The imprisoned companions were told that she planned to eventually settle with the small community of Japanese Christian converts living in Spanish Manila. The men could not have been happier to hear the news.

While relieved to hear about Keiko's safety, Lorenzo and the rest of his companions were anxious for news about what would happen to them. They were brought before

Okinawa's magistrate shortly after their arrest, but had heard nothing since. Days became weeks. Time dragged. No one knew what would happen next. All they could do was wait—and pray.

# Chapter 10

While Lorenzo, Lazaro, and the Dominican companions waited in the dark and dismal dungeon, the powerful territorial lord, the *daimyo* of Satsuma, and his advisers met in their chambers to decide the prisoners' fate. "Why has Okinawa insisted on referring this case to us?" the Satsuma *daimyo* demanded of his advisers. Months had passed since the documents on the case had been sent to him in Japan, along with the request for his opinion and ruling.

"These men are a mixed lot of foreigners—and some of our own people. It is, we should say, *complicated*," came the reply. "It is likely they wish to avoid any diplomatic blunders with us—or with China."

"But it is not as if the Ryukyuan courts have never decided cases involving foreigners, *sapposhi*, in the past," the *daimyo* noted. "These judgments have been clear-cut, and the executions swift. What about this is too delicate for the Ryukyuans, that they should refer this case to us?"

"It appears that the leper from Kyoto might have had some recognized status—that is, until he contracted the disease during the last war. After becoming a leper he was exiled to the Philippines, but returned with these missionaries, one of whom is a Japanese Catholic priest." This element piqued the *daimyo's* interest.

"His name? The priest, I mean."

"Vicente Shiwozuka de la Cruz."

" . . . unfamiliar to me," said the *daimyo* after a brief consultation with his aide. "But another question. Where did the leper's duties take him in the past, I wonder?"

"His father or grandfather might have served during the old Ashikaga shogunate, the former rulers in Kyoto. The leper has clearly been well educated and is fluent in at least three or four languages—our own tongue, Portuguese, Spanish, and a smattering of Chinese."

"I see. And his parents were—"

"Yes. They were Christian converts."

"This was why these men were all arrested, I presume? For the record, were they openly proselytizing, making converts, blatantly celebrating their religious ceremonies without regard for the shogun's edict to not participate in Christian ceremonies?"

"No," the adviser said flatly.

"Then how was their crime discovered?"

"An innkeeper reported their extended stay in her establishment."

"How long had they stayed there?"

"Thirty-six hours. Then three days later they were apprehended by Ryukyuan police."

"We don't want strangers settling in to make trouble. Was there any other wrongdoing?"

"That is all, for now."

"You fools, what do you take me for?" he retorted. "How do you expect me to make a decisive ruling on this case based on such flimsy evidence?"

The advisers paled and became visibly troubled.

"But, let us propose something, sir," one ventured respectfully.

"Yes? Such as?"

"If we wait out these men, they themselves will give us the evidence with which we can convict them. By watching them and their subsequent actions we will have everything we need to charge them with practicing, preaching, and promoting their faith."

"Clever. But I order that this case be elevated to the *bakufu's*[1] office in Edo instead," said the *daimyo*. "I'm sure he will appreciate the wisdom in the way the case is being handled, though it may take some time before we collect all the information needed. In any case, it will give us the time necessary to prosecute these men to the full extent of their guilt."

"And how much more time shall we allot them, sir?"

"How long have they already been held?"

"They have been in custody for four months now."

"Well, I suppose that they cannot hide any of their beliefs or practices much longer than that. Let us send this case to Edo by the end of the winter. How these missionaries endure prison will provide more than sufficient evidence to convict them."

"Very well, sir."

"Let it be so," the *daimyo* said officially, passing the case on and affixing his red-waxed seal on the documents.

But it took many more months before Edo's decision was handed down. In the meantime, the Dominicans, Lazaro, and Lorenzo listlessly lived their days of imprisonment like lost soldiers straggling to nowhere. Their plans had been cast to the wind and they had no idea of what lay in store.

Summer had come and gone. The stifling heat had

mellowed with the arrival of what the Ryukyuans called *miinishi*, cool air currents from the north. Outside their dungeon the people celebrated the autumn harvest. On the walls of their cells Lorenzo and the others felt the rhythmic beats of bass drums as the percussionists passed close by. Religious processions wound throughout the streets of the kingdom in celebration of the bountiful yield of the land for that year. All the prisoners could do was listen and wait.

Every day the Ryukyuan guards made a roll call of the inmates under their watch. It served as a reminder that they had not been forgotten. Some days, they were arbitrarily thrown into solitary confinement. It was during these trials of solitary imprisonment that the prisoners would sing out so as to accompany one another. This also allowed the European friars and their companions to determine where each one of them was—by the simple chant of Gregorian hymns. The familiar chants quieted and soothed the troubled spirits of the prisoners.

After months of not washing, all the prisoners were foul from the stench and were plagued with lice and open sores. The thick atmosphere had become so toxic that it was as if every breath they took choked them. Because of this, one day a large number of prisoners went into convulsions of coughing, leaving the guards with no choice but to empty the cells and move the majority of the inmates to another location while they investigated the source of this overpowering odor of decay.

To Father Antonio, this temporary upheaval represented a potential opportunity for their escape. He thought that they, too, would be moved and in that would lay their chance to regain their freedom. The jailers, however, had other plans for the Christian missionaries. While everyone else was let out, Lorenzo and the others were forced to clean the prison and rid it of the dead prisoners and the rats that had fed on their corpses. Theirs became an act of mercy for the dead as they searched cells and small niches for their decomposing bodies. Some men, not far from death and unable to fend for themselves or to move, were being eaten alive by feasting maggots and rats. Lorenzo and the others threw up upon seeing these inhumane conditions, soiling themselves with their own vomit and tears. Still, they plodded through until the onerous task was completed. The dead were removed from the jail and Father Antonio gathered the sick and the disabled along with those who were barely alive, so that a makeshift infirmary could be organized for their care.

Both fellow prisoners and the guards appreciated the new care-giving detail in the penitentiary. Each of the missionaries voluntarily took charge of one aspect of the needed care. Father Antonio coordinated the overall effort. Father Miguel took care of transporting the patients from their cells to the makeshift infirmary that had been set up in a separate section of the prison. Father Guillermo examined the patients and instructed others on how to dispense proper care. Lorenzo managed the meager food and water rations, assuring that those who were sick received at least a bowl of clear broth for meals. Previously, they had received nothing. Father Vicente accompanied those who were close to death, listening to their pleas and even a few confessions. And Lazaro of Kyoto took care of the mortuary and washed the bodies of those who had died. There were no burials; the corpses were simply cremated by the guards and the remains thrown into the sea.

# CHAPTER 11

The New Year ushered in an anticipation and hope of better things. As was their tradition the Ryukyuans met the occasion with the ceremonial rite of drawing water from their sacred stream. And it was with this water, which had been blessed by the Dominicans, that their prison surroundings were cleansed.

Father Miguel told some stories about the saints to the prisoners that the guards had summoned to assist the clerics. He took advantage of the fact that from talking about the saints it was not such a risky leap to speak about Christ himself. Without the benefit of liturgical books, the breviary, or the Bible, the Dominicans culled from memory long passages from Scripture, and shared what they remembered about the saints, especially Saint Dominic and Saint Francis. As a result, some of the prisoners entertained the thought of conversion. Others asked for Baptism shortly before they died. Lorenzo, the Dominicans, and Lazaro began to wonder if their missionary calling did not lie right where they were in their Ryukyuan prison.

"God works in mysterious ways," Father Antonio said.

"And he writes straight with crooked lines," Father Guillermo responded.

"It's a good thing *I* didn't use crooked lines," Lorenzo retorted. "You would never have made me your *escríbano*." They all smiled. In their current situation small blessings, and their deepening friendship, were things to be celebrated and the group made the most of them. But there were bigger blessings, too. Aided by clandestine Christians, who smuggled grape wine and unleavened wheat bread in portions small enough to be mistaken for doses of medicine, the priests were able to celebrate Mass in the prison several times. Although only baptized Catholics could receive Communion, the Presence of God was felt by others as well. The Eucharist seemed to draw them.

The care Lorenzo, Lazaro, and their Dominican friends provided had some of its deepest effects on Uehara, a native Ryukyuan from Okinawa. Though he denied it, some maintained that Uehara was a native shaman. He was known to be a nomad staying along the port, but he had withdrawn from regular contact with his neighbors after he had survived a near-fatal knifing. In any case Uehara's soothing presence helped to calm down many patients under the friars' care, even though he battled debilitating anxieties of his own.

Nonetheless, Uehara at first became Father Miguel's assistant in transporting the patients from the cells to the infirmary; later he worked his way into the tutelage of Father Guillermo in examining the patients and seeing to their proper care. At the more practical level, Father Vicente taught him a few methods of relaxation especially sought after in prayers for healing and daily regular intervals of meditation. Uehara was able to adapt to most of these, but letting go upset Uehara most. It was nearly impossible for him to surrender anything, including the fear that gripped and controlled him. Sometimes when situations in the dispensary became especially hectic, Uehara was seized with an acute form of terror. This could result in his being incapacitated the entire day. The constancy and flow of prayer that Uehara learned from Father Vicente helped to reduce both the occasions and the severity of these terror and panic attacks.

Lorenzo was happy to see his companions help someone like Uehara, and offer him the same kindness and assistance they had given him. *Truly, there is something beautiful seeing those weighed down by their crosses help others to get up after a fall,* he thought. *I will offer one of my Rosaries for him, and ask the Mother of God for her assistance.*

He fingered his beads almost without thinking. In the rhythm of prayer, Lorenzo found a kind of freedom. During prayer his soul could wander outside the prison walls and beyond the confines of his terrible situation. Lorenzo would often imagine himself just outside the door of his family's home. He could picture himself peeking through the window there, and he would see a sight that stole his breath. His daughter and two sons had grown so much since he had last seen them. He hoped they would remember him and not think he had left them and their mother to fend for themselves. "I am far away, but my heart is still with you," Lorenzo whispered. He wondered if they could somehow hear him. Yes, prayer was a refuge for Lorenzo and his companions as well as for their fellow prisoners like Uehara who were benefitting from the peace that comes with talking and listening to God in prayer.

The need for what the Dominicans, Lorenzo, and Lazaro provided was acute. Few trained doctors cared to take up the cases of those imprisoned; with everything else happening on the island the sick and malnourished prisoners were hardly a priority. The superintendent of guards, however, could see the practical value of tending to the prisoners' needs and discussed the matter at length with Father Antonio. It was agreed that the Dominicans would run the hospital ward as a mission, without any compensation save for their possible release from prison. The superintendent would speak in their favor with the Ryukyuan magistrate. This possibility was the best news that the little group from the Philippines had received in the eight months since they were detained.

～～

So it was that the Dominicans, Lorenzo, and Lazaro continued to care for the ailing prisoners offering them comfort and gentle treatment. Time passed since the "deal" was made with the guard superintendent. It was now spring and shoots were breaking through the ground and the natives of Okinawa were celebrating the festival of insects in preparation for the planting season. Lorenzo, Lazaro, and the priests continued to give the best possible care to the inmates, but by the end of spring in 1637, hopes for their eventual release dimmed. While they waited for a decision from the Ryukyuan magistrate, they received the news that their case had been reassigned to Nagasaki, in Japan. It was the worst of their fears—Christians were treated even more harshly in Japan than in Okinawa.

Lorenzo and his companions fell silent. They had been imprisoned in Okinawa for nearly a year. The superintendent was apologetic, even openly regretful that events had not developed differently. Even the superintendent recognized that these men who treated their fellow prisoners with such tenderness and love would receive harsher treatment in Japan than he cared to imagine. All he could offer them was a promise to treat them with gratitude and some leniency during the remainder of their stay in Okinawa. He also advised them to be ready to depart for Japan with hardly any notice.

The men looked at each other, and without uttering a single word each shared similar thoughts. Any attempt to escape was out of the question, because if they managed to escape the superintendent who had been so kind to them would be held responsible and possibly pay with his life.

The news affected not only Lorenzo, Lazaro, and the priests but also their fellow prisoners. Uehara went into a panic punctuated by weeping and wailing that lasted several days. Despite their own dire circumstances, the priests, Lorenzo, and Lazaro continued to help the other prisoners and in particular to help Uehara. Through prayer he was purged of all he could possibly fear for the meantime, and slowly came to accept the fact that his newfound friends would be leaving. Though disengaged from regular conversation, Uehara managed to smile when any of the priests spoke to him. Together the men prayed Psalm 23.

> The LORD is my shepherd,
> I shall not want;
> He makes me lie down in green pastures.
> He leads me beside still waters;
> He restores my soul.
> He leads me in right paths for his name's sake.
> Even though I walk through the darkest valley,
> I fear no evil;
> For you are with me;
> Your rod and your staff—
> They comfort me.
> You prepare a table before me
> in the presence of my enemies;
> You anoint my head with oil,
> my cup overflows.
> Surely goodness and mercy shall follow

me all the days of my life;
And I shall dwell in the house
of the LORD my whole life long.

The dreaded day arrived in late summer. The prisoners, who were now held in high esteem by the guards and the other prisoners, were being transported to Japan to await their fate. The Ryukyuan guards escorted the Dominican company as well as Lazaro and Lorenzo through the celebrated *Shureimon* gate, which heralded welcomed guests into the "Land of Propriety." Though the party of six had not at first been welcome, their send-off was marked by a deep reverence for them. Coming from somewhere far off in the background toward the castle, Father Vicente heard the sound of singing. A choir of prisoners was offering up a Gregorian chant for their beloved friars.

It was a matter of tradition for native Okinawans to wait at the gate to welcome wise elders and highly esteemed teachers. Strangely, crowds converged there in great numbers this day to honor and bid the six missionaries farewell. Father Antonio made the sign of the cross, blessing the assembly. "Remember us in your prayers!" he exclaimed. "For we are all children of the one true God. My one regret is that, as your brothers, we could not stay long enough to tell you of his boundless mercy." Wanting to leave them with something to live by, Father Antonio continued, "Just bear in mind—and especially in your hearts—that you will never ever regret a decision that is conceived and delivered from real love."

With that they marched in silence to the Japanese ship awaiting them at dockside. Immediately, they recognized that their fate lay in the hands of the one man who stood before them. He came dressed in full samurai regalia, with battle gear, armor, and the colors of Nagasaki both at his side and atop the ship's mast. Father Vicente wondered if the samurai was not a little bit overdressed for the arrest of six unarmed, lightly clothed prisoners who put up no resistance. The proceedings had a formality about them, however, and all stood at attention during the turnover. As the samurai barked orders to his underlings, the prisoners remained tied and gagged, defenseless against the plans of men, but resigned to the will of the God who had brought them this far.

On his face Lorenzo felt a slight brush of the cool *miinishi* winds returning from the north. He noted with some gladness that they would not pass another winter in Okinawa. But he failed to consider what winter might be like on the Japanese mainland.

# Jomei, the Samurai

# CHAPTER 12

Jomei did not take off his samurai helmet until after the Japanese *fune* had cleared the last sight of the Okinawa kingdom and the sail had been completely hoisted. Wiping his brow, he kept thinking about how inconvenient this encounter was. Jomei sat down on deck facing his prisoners, who had been positioned in a semicircle against the foremast, bound and under guard. He proceeded to unburden himself of armor.

"These prisoners must be visible at every moment of our voyage," Jomei ordered. "There can be no possible way for any of them to escape."

"Yes, sir," one of the guards answered. "There will be no trouble."

"There is *always* trouble with Christians!" Jomei barked back, "and this mixed band of foreigners promises to be even worse. Which one of you speaks Japanese?"

Both Father Vicente and Lazaro looked up and nodded.

"Tell my orders to the others, then, and do it precisely."

The guard began to speak again, but Jomei, obviously agitated, continued.

"Catholics, Lutherans, Reformed, Presbyterian—we have seen their petty squabbles become great wars in their own lands." Jomei's voice was raised now, and his frustration was evident. "Japan has no need for such nonsense. Those who listen to their teachings are fools."

The Dominican companions looked at each other with surprise. None of them would have imagined that a pagan soldier in the Far East would have known very much about Christian factions and their disputes. Listening to Lazaro translate, Lorenzo was impressed that the samurai knew more about Christian Europe than he did. He was obviously intelligent as well as hostile and made his loyalties clear from the start without misgivings.

Jomei handed the last bit of his armor to an assistant, then turned to face his prisoners. "But," he said calmly, "we are alike in two important ways." The men's eyes met intently. "We do not split our allegiances; you serve your master and I, mine. And second, none of us would hesitate to take our loyalty to the furthest limits of what we can bear." Somehow, his words held the force of threat.

Jomei studied each one of his charges, beginning with Father Antonio. It was almost as if he knew the station of every man in this small grouping instinctively. Eventually, his eyes fell on Lorenzo, whom he deemed the least important among them. After his own assessments of them were complete, Jomei unfurled the scrolls of information and evidence against each man, to check if his conclusions matched the record.

Walking toward the ship's prow, he turned around, and with his back against the sun, spoke from behind them.

"Untie them," Jomei ordered two of his guards. They hesitated and the samurai repeated himself with some irritation. "Go on, untie them." The prisoners had grown listless after being tied up for several hours. Ordering them to face him, Jomei demanded their full attention. But the prisoners barely moved from their positions on the deck floor. One guard slapped Father Miguel with the back of his hand until the cleric's nose bled, another angrily kicked Father Guillermo in the shins. This elicited some response. But although each of them was subjected to various degrees of abuse, still hardly a groan arose from them. To Jomei it seemed that the men were testing his resolve. If that were the case he would have no choice but to make a fierce display of it. Suddenly, he stomped toward Father Vicente and gave him a great wallop on the left side of his head. The priest began to bleed from the ear.

"According to these documents you are all guilty of performing works of charity," he said. "Obviously, this is no crime," he concluded. "But know this: whatever connivance you may have had with the Ryukyuans will not serve you in a Nagasaki court; you can be assured of that." Jomei then ordered a lower-ranking officer to loosen the restraints on the captives' mouths. After some short dispute with this first officer, the command was carried out. The man was relieved from present duty and relegated below deck. The friars observed that there appeared to be something Jomei wanted to get off his chest. It was clear that he was not going to let policies or procedures hamper his intent. Being alone with Jomei was something they had not expected.

In any case, conversation was something that animated them, even under their present duress.

"Excuse me, sir, but what kind of dealings have you had with the Protestants?" Father Antonio asked through Father Vicente.

"Your skirmishes with them have become common knowledge, especially for those in Nagasaki." He was referring to the presence of the Dutch in the small island of

Dejima, just off the city's harbor. Like many of the Europeans, the Dutch had played one Christian faction against another to advance their own interests in Japan.

"Frankly, I do not understand how one Christian group is any better than another," Jomei said. "Why do we Japanese tolerate any of this? I have seen many Christians, all of them sorry and weak like yourselves, and I wonder, what do we in Japan have to fear?" He laughed ever more scornfully as if the remark might humor his captives. "You cannot imagine that you will invade an empire such as Japan with a leper for a recruit," he said referring to Lazaro of Kyoto. "How you have conquered the Philippines, I can only wonder," he said to Father Antonio. "Unless *you*," Jomei said pointing derisively at Lorenzo, "unless you and your countrymen have not yet been roused from sleep." Lorenzo's mind flashed to Manila. Much to his dismay, his memory of home had begun to fade. At least he could still see Rosario and the children in his mind's eye.

"Nonetheless, I am not one to underestimate my foes. The Spanish have conquered much of the world. But their dirty tricks will not reach our shores because we Japanese prefer a clean house," he said, picking up grime on his fingertips as he ran them atop the rail. "We rid ourselves of sore parasites. We could be rid of you now as well, but we need to draw out the pests in our own shores. This is why we are here together, so that we can make examples of you and end this Catholic encroachment among our people once and for all."

"We are hardly the threat you describe," protested Father Antonio. "It is not as if we can even pull ourselves up from the floor. And yet great is the Lord Jesus Christ who does so much with so little. It is a testament to his power and goodness."

Jomei was infuriated with what Father Antonio had said, and his deckhands pretended not to have heard it. But his honor required him to rebut the priest's assertions lest he lose face before his men. So, Jomei ordered that the prisoners be bound up once more and gagged before he offered a reply. As soon as his orders were carried out, Jomei addressed the prisoners.

"We can end this pretense even now," Jomei continued. ". . . if you renounce your foolish faith in a dead God," he said as if he were outlining the rubrics for their salvation. "Nod and we will all be rid of these fears and threats. Agree that you will leave this Christ aside and serve the Japanese people another way. This is not outside of what you believe of charity." The priests looked at the samurai. But their reactions perplexed him. Jomei suspected that his was not the first lure that someone had dangled before them. He decided to make it clear that it would not be the last threat either.

"Unless you do as I suggest, you will be judged. And after the sentence has been handed down . . . ," he trailed rather clumsily to a silence. "When you are sentenced you will have wished that you had considered the anguish you might have avoided."

The lack of expression in his voice intensified Lorenzo's horror at what he was hearing.

"Be assured, priests, that if you do not recant, you will experience torments beyond imagining," he continued. "And death for you will be of slight consolation. We call it the suffering that leaves welts upon the ground. There will be little respite."

The awkwardness that accompanied the warnings served a double purpose for the samurai. It was as if by making a mental documentation of the proceedings he was able to give fair warning, but also justify his own actions later.

"Therefore I say to you what the Romans said to the first of Christ's believers: 'A religion which adores a crucified man cannot be good,'" Jomei said.

Father Antonio and the rest studied Jomei intently. A door into this man's core had been left ajar, Father Antonio determined, and he, a priest, had been allowed to gain some guarded, hallowed access. It was obvious to Lorenzo that this was not the samurai's first hearing of God's sacred Word. But how it had metastasized into this malignancy and hatred—or why—he could only guess. Was Jomei himself, or someone dear to him, a Christian apostate—perhaps one who had been severely tortured into renouncing the faith? Was he searching for ways to rationalize that decision?

After some persistent mumbling through clenched teeth, Jomei allowed the Dominican superior to have his say and loosened the gag on his mouth. "However scornful it may seem to you, we must insist on the cross. It is not that we seek death alone," continued Father Antonio, "but that because of the resurrection of our Lord from the dead and his ascension into heaven we will have eternal life. There is victory in the cross because God has defeated death through it." Jomei shook his head as the priest continued. Lorenzo thought he sounded almost as if he were preaching at Mass. "If all you see is death and destruction, I am sorry for you. The cross of Jesus Christ is a passage, and not an end, a means and not a goal. It is evident even in the laws of nature. A tree takes up its nourishment from the earth that becomes a part of it. God, who is almighty, became man to take us up into himself, to raise us from our petty evil nature. The cross is planted in the earth, absorbing our sins and making all things new in Christ, the Redeemer of all creation."

"You speak nonsense and riddles, priest," Jomei retorted. "Of what use is this cross to me?"

"You are only confirming what Saint Paul wrote. The 'message about the cross is foolishness to those who are perishing, but to us who are being saved it is the power of God.'"[1]

"In other words, you don't know," Jomei sneered. "Wasn't it one of you priests who said that faith was a gift? Well, this God of yours has not given it to me. But that doesn't matter because I have no use for it. What does matter is here and now," he said brandishing his weapon as if he could slice the very breath of his speech. "And this should matter more to you than anything else because your lives depend on it from here on."

"What we have comes to us from above," replied Father Antonio, referring to the words of Christ to Pontius Pilate, the Roman procurator who judged Jesus and sent him to death.

"You speak of Christ crucified and yet I wonder about those who had him put to death. What do you say about the men who carried out the law and fulfilled their duties to the state?"

"Jesus did not come to break the law but to fulfill it. What matters to Christ is what you hold dear in your heart, the purity of your intentions, the charity you have for your brothers and sisters. Regardless of what or who you believe in, this is the measure to which we are all held."

"But you are not my brother, and we were not talking about me" Jomei said in a blatant attempt to end the discourse.

"In Christ and in truth, we are all brothers."

At this the samurai laughed. "What I will be required to do to you can hardly be considered brotherly," he answered. "You can let me hear your kind words when I am through."

Jomei thrust his chest forward like a preening

peacock and strode toward the stern, leaving the prisoners hand-tied and bound on the deck floor, and Father Antonio silenced once more with restraints. *The shogun is right to be afraid of all this,* Jomei thought. *This God, he wins their heart even as he breaks it. Yet they know it and are joyful to the point of real hope. What fools. What sorry, sorry fools. Of what possible use is their suffering? What kind of God deals in such useless currency?*

# Nagasaki

# Chapter 13

After a week of traveling the coastline the Japanese *fune* stopped over at the port of Kagoshima, on the southern tip of the island of Kyushu and not far from the city of Nagasaki. It was curious to the prisoners that Jomei chose to spend a night here. Kagoshima was the center of Christian activity in Japan. The Jesuit missionary Francis Xavier had landed here in 1549. It was in Kagoshima that the hearts of the very first Japanese converts had been won to the Catholic faith.

As Jomei once again assessed his charges, he decided to split the men into two groups. Fathers Guillermo Courtet, Miguel de Aozaraza, and Vicente Shiwozuka de la Cruz sailed for Nagasaki with Jomei, and arrived there on September 13, 1637.[1] The second group, headed by Father Antonio Gonzalez, included Lazaro of Kyoto and Lorenzo Ruiz. They made a stopover on Dejima Island off the narrow inlet of Nagasaki Harbor a week later, and didn't arrive in the city until September 21, 1637.

Though Lorenzo wasn't there to see it, he later discovered that Jomei and his group of prisoners did not enter Nagasaki quietly. Disembarking from the *fune* at the center of the wharf, Jomei paraded the Dominican captives shamelessly through the busiest section of the city on foot. From the pier, vendors in their storefronts shoveled pallets of dough into their ovens, providing the Dominicans with a generous whiff of warm baked bread, the kind that the Portuguese called *pao*, and sponge cakes that Japanese women sold in the streets as *kasutera. Some foreign things are not so easily gotten rid of,* thought Father Miguel. It had been a very long time since any of them had savored anything fresh and the delicious aromas were a bit of torture to the malnourished and hungry prisoners. Father Vicente kept his head bowed, following behind Father Guillermo like a scolded child. The Japanese were suspicious of strangers, especially if they were foreigners. Some of the locals even hurled taunts and jeered at them.

It seemed as if the Gospel had not made a lasting good impression here. Any memory of it seemed to have been erased by increasing persecution, and in its place came the din of rejection, both of the faith and of those who would follow it. "What great deeds could be accomplished here," Father Miguel whispered to himself, "if the faith were sown and cultivated within the soul of every person." Knowing what he knew of God's love and mercy, how could he offer them anything less than the beauty of this sublime truth? "They have eyes but do not see," he said to himself. The faith had once been cultivated openly and freely here, but even in persecution, it would prosper by God's grace. For anyone who knew it in mind and heart, never lived the same existence again. Faith elevated the believer beyond the material and the tangible, Father Miguel knew. As they continued what was supposed to be a parade of shame he looked at each person along the paths of Nagasaki as a brother or sister. As he pondered how little time they had left to preach to them, he wept. "If you, even you, had only recognized on this day the things that make for peace," he prayed for Nagasaki, quoting the

Lord as he had entered Jerusalem that Palm Sunday, sixteen centuries before. "But now they are hidden from your eyes. Indeed, the days will come upon you, when your enemies will set up ramparts around you and surround you, and hem you in on every side. They will crush you to the ground, you and your children within you, and they will not leave within you one stone upon another; because you did not recognize the time of your visitation from God."[2]

After more than a year in a Ryukyu prison, the three Dominicans that Jomei brought to Nagasaki were surprised by how swiftly they were called to appear before the Japanese court. Even before being taken to a Nagasaki jail and without waiting for the other three prisoners to arrive they were herded before two Japanese *bugyos*, or magistrates, jointly appointed by the shogun to administer the government in Nagasaki. These *bugyos* originated from the samurai class and were clothed as such. With formal dark kimonos, broad shoulders overlaid with black robes, and their hairlines receding into a knot of hair high on their scalps, their appearance was imposing.

In haste, Jomei had not bothered to give his prisoners a change of clothing, not even for the event of their trial. So, they stood before the court as they were—dirty and pungent, a flawless reflection of their long imprisonment and harsh, inhumane treatment as prisoners.

"Who are you?" asked the older *bugyo* Sakakibara Hida-no-kami, addressing the group as if he were speaking to a single man.

No one answered.

"Do you speak Japanese?"

Still, no response.

"Bring an interpreter," the *bugyo* demanded impatiently.

"Who are you?" asked the interpreter.

"We are Catholic religious priests of the Order of Saint Dominic," replied Father Guillermo, the oldest of the clerics, who assumed the role of spokesman. Throughout their incarceration he had not lost the bearing of his French nobility, though the slight stoop of his shoulders betrayed his age. "One of us, Father Vicente, was not a Dominican priest when we met him," he continued. "But he entered our order when he decided to come to Japan."

"How long ago did you leave Manila?"

"One year ago."

"Didn't you know that there is a prohibition forbidding missionaries to come to Japan?"

"Yes. Not only we, but everyone knows about it. In spite of this, we have come to ransom souls and to show them the way of salvation, to the small and the innocent as well as adults and even renegades."

Unmoved, the *bugyo* Sakakibara proceeded through an interpreter.

"Do you know how to speak Japanese?"

"No, we don't. Father Miguel started to study the language when he was chosen for this mission, and he understands a little bit."

"Did the Governor of Manila send you here?"

"No, he didn't. On the contrary, had he known of our departure he would have prevented it. Only our Dominican Provincial Superior had knowledge of it. Nobody else."

Two court transcribers made efficient note of the Dominican's responses. The *bugyo* continued. "In what boat did you come and who brought you?"

"We had a boat constructed for this purpose, but the Governor was informed and he ordered the boat to be burned. Then we decided to come in a sampan."

"Have you received letters from someone in Japan inviting you to come or promising to shelter you or to help you by giving you alms?"

"No one but God has called us to come here, nor do we know anyone in this land, much less anyone who can shelter us. We came from Spain to the Philippines very recently. Our sole purpose was to pass through to China and Japan, and to teach the people about Jesus Christ and the way of salvation. Our plan was to go to the mountains and stay hidden until perhaps some remaining Christians or other persons would offer us some accommodations."

The younger magistrate, Baba Saburozayemon, raised his gaze to look at the men and disinterestedly continued the interrogation. "Did the Portuguese of Macao help you to send letters to Japan or to receive any correspondence from here?"

"No, we know nothing about the Portuguese. And we do not expect anything from them."

The older Sakakibara butted in. "Did you bring money with you or did you hope to receive some here?"

This time, Father Miguel replied through the interpreter, "I bring a *pan de oro*[3] in my shoes. And Father Guillermo brings a *manila*.[4] Father Antonio Gonzalez, our superior who is with the rest of our group, gave us a *barra de oro*[5] divided into four pieces. All this money is intended for the expenses of our whole group. We also brought 100 pesos for our immediate needs, which we spent in Okinawa."

"What are the names of your superiors?"

"Our Provincial Superior is Father Domingo Gonzalez," Father Miguel answered. "The superior of our monastery of Santo Domingo is Father Francisco de Herrera. And the superior who accompanies us is Father Antonio Gonzalez. A Filipino who accompanies this superior of ours came with us. He is a Chinese-Filipino mestizo from Manila who could not stay there, and believing that he could make a living in Macao, came with us. Lorenzo Ruiz is a skilled *escríbano* and could prosper there. But then he chose to come with us to Japan."

"Did you bring additional clothes to wear in Japan?"

"Yes, some *kimonos* were given to us by our community."

Noticing Father Guillermo's fair complexion and blond hair, the Japanese judges queried him about a possible connection with the Dutch on Dejima Island. "Do you intend to live with the Dutch and preach Christianity to them?"

"My concern is for Japanese Christians, those who now live their faith in secret. I planned to live in the mountains, give them the sacraments, and teach the way of salvation to these children and the innocent." said Father Guillermo.

"Are you a theologian?"

"Yes, I am a theologian and a professor of theology. And my companion Father Miguel is a very good theologian, too, although he is not a professor."

The younger magistrate Baba Saburozayemon continued. "Is there a seminary in Manila for teaching the Japanese language and training Japanese priests? And if so, were there many ordained and have many of them passed through China with the intention of coming to Japan dressed as Chinese?"

"A seminary of sorts was started for that purpose and some were ordained priests. But none of them passed through China."

The dispassionate interrogation ended and the priests were taken aside. The *bugyos* folded their fans perfunctorily and slipped them into their sleeves as they exited into another chamber. It was only after the swift session had come to a close that the clerics took any notice of their surroundings. Jomei sat facing the judges' seats as if they were still present in the room. He appeared to be rehearsing a line or two just in case he was called upon to make a statement.

But what caught the Dominicans' interest were the two transcribers or translators, both of whom were quite well versed in Spanish. Obviously, they had been well educated and taken pains to translate the priests' replies with much care and thought. Intent on their task, they deliberated and compared notes of the Dominicans' responses between queries, and continued to do so even after the *bugyos* had left the chamber. Father Guillermo could not shake the notion that these translators might be Christians who had fallen away from the faith. Father Vicente became convinced of it, however, when he saw the healed gash on the head of the translator, just above the left ear. It was the scar of one who had been hung from his feet into a pit, an extreme form of Japanese torture that bled the victim slowly as he died from suffocation. Rumors of it were widespread across Asia. The accused hung until they died or chose to renounce their faith, using a free hand to signal remorse and surrender. It became known as the most notorious form of punishment against Catholic Christians anywhere. Father Vicente reeled at the thought and began to heave.

Prevented from conferring among themselves, the three Dominican clerics stood separately, each man isolated from the other, absorbed in his own thoughts, worries, and prayers.

*How much could they endure?* wondered Father Miguel. Father Vicente, distraught by what he imagined would be their impending torture, fell to his knees in a profuse sweat and made an unsuccessful bid to contain his trembling. Father Guillermo prayed silently.

After brief deliberation the *bugyos* returned to the chamber and handed their decision to one of the court officers. The verdict was read aloud in Japanese by one translator and again in Spanish for the benefit of the accused.

"By virtue of the existing laws of the land (*sasoku*), the edicts of 1614 and of 1632 (the extinction of Christianity and the closure of Japan to the outer world), you three priests are hereby found guilty from the moment when you affirmed yourselves to be Catholic priests and religious, and are sentenced to death. Only one thing can save you from execution. That is a complete renunciation of your faith forcibly obtained by torture."[6]

# CHAPTER 14

At this cue Jomei sprang into action and ushered his charges to the torture chamber across from the court. He was eager to be done with the whole thing and to complete the distasteful task that belonged to him. The mere display of the torture devices weakened Father Vicente into early submission. To the consternation and disappointment of his Dominican brother priests, Father Vicente immediately opted to apostasize.

"How may I save this miserable life of mine and avoid the plagues of torture?" he cried out to his accusers. But the *bugyo* ordered that Father Vicente be tortured nevertheless as punishment for his betrayal of the Japanese customs. In fact, he prescribed a lengthier and harsher penalty for the Japanese cleric.

Father Guillermo thought of the mockery of a trial that they had just been made to withstand, a drastic departure from the torture they were about to undergo. Father Miguel thought of little else but survival. He knew himself too well and felt he could not even pretend that he had been made of the stuff of martyrs. He was only a priest coming to serve the faithful. Of what use was he dead to the few remaining

Christians in Nagasaki? "We were to live in the mountains," he mumbled to himself, "waiting for the Christians to come to us. What possible threat was there in this ascetic way of life? Spare us, O Lord. Spare us." What Father Miguel could not avoid noticing was how utterly beautiful the day was, with a clear blue sky outside—and hardly a cloud to mar his vision during the short duration of the walk they made from the court into this dark room, reeking with the odor of bile and blood.

Father Vicente was both shaken and shamed by his own weakness. The bright day outside and the darkness of the cell were virtually indistinguishable to him. Noticing nothing around him, all he thought about was how much he had wanted to serve his fellow Japanese Christians, and yet how easily he had turned from Jesus. Consumed by thoughts of what had just transpired, he wondered when he had begun to lose his faith. *Was it when I failed to forgive a petty annoyance? Or enviously considered a life other than this one? Was it when I toyed with the emotions of a young woman?* Something had made him waiver in his resolve when it mattered most and Father Vicente felt the weight of his dishonor. Glancing for a moment at Father Miguel and Father Guillermo, the broken priest prayed both for God's forgiveness and the strength to endure. Then his prayers took a different turn, toward the three companions they had left behind: Father Antonio, Lazaro of Kyoto, and Lorenzo Ruiz. "What of the others?" he said quietly.

All three priests closed their eyes. They could only imagine answers to the questions that stirred their hearts. *Where were Father Antonio, Lazaro, and Lorenzo in this vast unwelcoming terrain? What possible torments might they be undergoing?* Somehow, thinking about their companions took their own fear away from them for the briefest instant.

It also brought them to a depth of intercessory prayer they had never experienced before.

But praying for their companions was not the only depth they would discover that day. The profundity of human suffering and the kind of cruelty it took to usher someone there was but moments away.

~~~

Despite their extreme suffering, the priests kept their heads lifted up throughout their torture. Under Jomei's command the tormentors did everything they could to induce them to renounce the faith. But to the consternation of the *bugyos*, none—including Father Vicente—had done so.

"Like Christ's agony in the garden," cried out Father Miguel, as he began to pray the Way of the Cross. "My Father, if it is possible, let this cup pass from me," he begged. "Yet not what I want but what you want."[1]

For the three priests the day ended with barely any awareness of time, but their existence became excruciatingly acute. A mere brush on the skin brought about convulsions of extreme pain. Especially feverish and sharp was the soreness of their internal organs. Their throats turned raspy from blood and bile. Even their hearing became impaired, as if talking through an internal echo.

The next day, September 14, they endured much of the same all over again. Father Guillermo lost consciousness first, and then Father Miguel. But doubting the endurance of Father Vicente, Jomei continued the brutality without pause until he and his men tired themselves and ceased the proceedings. Like soiled rags, the priests were hoisted onto the pallets of their agony and thrown into a dungeon. They lay as they had the previous evening—in separate cells, with a thin wood panel separating one cell from the other. Only their skin kept the pulp of their sinews from sloughing off their bones. It was as if their bodies were being wrenched from their souls. But life prevailed in the tenuous connections of tissues and veins. Every throbbing cell of their bodies pulsed with life, and why it had not yet ceased was a wonder.

In soft, barely audible voices the Dominicans chanted a thanksgiving that another day had elapsed with none of them given over to apostasy. Father Guillermo offered a fitting passage from Psalm 22. "I am poured out like water, and all my bones are out of joint; my heart is like wax; it is melted within my breast; my mouth is dried up like a potsherd, and my tongue sticks to my jaws; you lay me in the dust of death."[2]

Because of their severe injuries the Dominicans could not be roused the following morning, so Jomei and his men employed another variation of torture. On September 15, they hung each man from his feet, and at intervals submerged his head into a water-filled barrel bringing them to the precipice of drowning and suffocation. When the Dominicans returned to consciousness, Jomei proceeded with still more inhumane torture. The three priests were brought before the officials of the court and the executioners. Taken outside, each priest was made to sit on a chair. With their feet fettered to the legs of the chair, their hands were bound and crossed before their chests. The executioners then took long needles and thrust a needle into each fingertip of the priests between the flesh and the nail. This however was not the end of the torture. The priests were then ordered to scrape the wall as if playing a guitar; this increased the pain each felt exponentially.[3]

The vicious spasm it produced surpassed the bewilderment the clerics had for such a diabolical form of torture. This was outside the previous range of their endurance. If they had borne the earlier water torture largely in silence because they had struggled for breath, the torment of the needles extracted soul-wrenching declarations of anguish.

Each victim suffered the pains of this torture differently. Father Guillermo said many things, enumerating all his sins aloud for everyone to hear and begging the Lord each time for forgiveness. He cried out repeatedly until he exhausted all efforts, but found no repose. Father Miguel smiled in absolute resignation and paradoxical defiance. And with his eye trained above into the unexplored cosmos, he uttered beautiful words of devotion to the Blessed Lady and the Lord. Father Vicente, however, could not bear the imposition and like a raging lion, he fought off the executioners with brisk madness. Jomei reinforced his team with up to thirty men to restrain the Japanese cleric until they inserted every last needle into his bleeding fingertips.

The infernal screaming of the priest brought tears even to Jomei's eyes, but seeing Father Vicente's sentimentality emboldened him to new heights of cruelty. This was beyond any strength that Father Vicente had managed to hold in his heart, and desperate to end the pain he gave in to the temptation of apostasy.

"I renounce. I renounce this faith," he cried, "and all its pains, and all its hardships, and all its false and foolish promises."

# CHAPTER 15

The on-looking *bugyos* were pleased, especially be-cause the priest who had recanted was a native Japanese. But Father Miguel and Father Guillermo were seized by the hor-ror of what renouncing Christ would mean for their compan-ion's soul. They prayed aloud together, over and above the desperate oaths Father Vicente was making to the Japanese authorities.

Somehow, perhaps by some miracle, Father Vicente realized what he had been saying. Suddenly, as if filled with newfound strength, he reconsidered what he was doing and fully gave himself over to the sacrifice. Calling out the name of the Blessed Mother, she who was pierced in her heart with every form of suffering, he repented of turning his back on his faith and embraced the cross. In that moment Father Vi-cente's mind was enlightened and he realized the power of this currency called suffering—a curse in itself, but given worth by the Son of God because he entered into it. With outstretched arms Christ had saved the world, and breathed his divine mercy upon all who betrayed him.

Father Vincent's eyes fell upon Jomei. It was the face of a samurai warrior, of honor lived out as he was trained to understand it. Near delirium Father Vicente fell into meditating on how the seven *bushido* virtues every samurai strove for might correspond to the virtues of the devout disciple of Jesus Christ. Right decisions, valor, benevolence, respect, honesty, honor, and loyalty: these *bushido* values were not exclusive to Japan. He had seen them lived out by his companions who shared his sufferings.

Father Vicente concluded as he looked into the eyes of his foes that Catholicism also embraced and went beyond those values that Jomei and the other samurais held dear. For Catholics and all Christians no virtue was true unless it emanated from a spirit of charity. No one can claim righteousness if he goes against his brother or sister, demeaning the very essence of what it means to be human. His faith had taught him that the primary value is charity or love: love for God and love of neighbor. It was not as if he needed proof of this, or that he had not understood the lesson before in Scripture. But, perhaps because of the prayers of his brother priests, Father Vicente had now absorbed the meaning into his being.

Day after day the physically weakened friars faced their tormentors. The Dominicans had come to accept the invitation before them. They knew the Lord was mysteriously calling them to an extreme form of sacrifice. It was for the benefit of their souls and those who did not yet know God. They took their cue from what Jesus said, "If any want to become my followers, let them deny themselves and take up their cross and follow me. For those who want to save their life will lose it, and those who lose their life for my sake and for the sake of the gospel, will save it. For what will it profit them to gain the whole world and forfeit their life?"[1]

On Thursday, September 21, the three Dominican priests were yanked from their cells in the early morning mist and marched to the port. It was dark when they started out and a cock crowed in the distance. Shuffling along on the path leading to the shore, they towed the line that tethered them to one another by their ankles, hands, and necks. Their heads remained bowed until they joined the crowds of busy people along the pier. As chickens fretted in their basket cages, the priests were the object of near constant mocking and ridicule from passersby. Father Miguel thought how disconcerting it was to observe people being quite preoccupied with the mundane demands of life and then pausing in an afterthought to spit at him and the other priests.

About the only goodness they relished was having the sun rising behind them, bathing them in the warmth of its rays. The rolling hills of Nagasaki with Mt. Mubonzan towering above seemed to extend a protective embrace around the harbor. Father Guillermo closed his eyes and took in the scent of the sea and fresh air.

By ten o'clock Jomei had begun pacing back and forth. His agitation seemed to stem from the sight of a particular Japanese *fune* that had pulled into the small island of Dejima, just off Nagasaki Harbor. In a short while three prisoners disembarked from the ship, looking like lost children in a forest of ships' masts. The missionary group was reunited as Father Antonio, Lazaro of Kyoto, and Lorenzo Ruiz stepped cautiously toward Fathers Guillermo, Miguel, and Vicente. The new arrivals appeared well compared to their companions, and Lorenzo wondered to himself: *What fear has filled their eyes? What have they endured?* Father Antonio maintained a calm, purposeful exterior as he stepped forward and searched the wan expressions of his brothers. Concluding the worst, he crossed himself in the name of the most Holy Trinity. A Dutch captain scoffed at the friars and ordered the remaining pair of captives to move along.

By decree, the residents of Nagasaki were obliged to witness the public transfer of prisoners and if necessary, their final sentence on Nishizaka Hill. Public spectacles on Nishizaka Hill served as deterrents to would-be and secret believers in Christ. It also allowed the captives a final chance to recant before they died. Some of those who did renounce their faith did in time physically heal and recover, but they were never quite the same. Those who recanted and survived attested to the great pains they had suffered in the worst device of torture ever permitted by the Japanese *bugyos*—the pit of the *ana-tsurushi*.[2]

The group was again separated. The new arrivals were driven into the courtroom. The remaining clerics were detained in cells across from them.

There were a number of attendees in the courtroom this time. The *bugyos* had invited three well-regarded guests—all former priests who had renounced their faith. Two of them were Japanese. The other, a tall European dressed in a black kimono, had his hair tied back in Japanese fashion. The clean-shaven European was Cristovao Ferreira, age fifty-seven, a controversial figure and former head of the Jesuits in Japan. Under the shogun's repressive rule, he had been captured and tortured four years ago. When he was captured Ferreira had already been a missionary in Japan for nearly twenty-four years, having arrived in 1609. But to the shame of his Jesuit brothers, he had recanted his faith after only six hours of torture in the pit of the *ana-tsurushi*. And only a year ago he had published a book denouncing Christianity. Written from the perspective of an insider, some believed his captors had coerced him into authoring it. In any case he had been given a Japanese name—Sawano Chuan, as well as a Japanese wife.

Father Antonio trained a determined Spanish gaze at the Portuguese Ferreira, praying in silence that the fallen priest return to the fold. Ferreira acknowledged the Dominican's presence with a slight bow and then turned with a courteous second nod toward the *bugyos*.

Sensing a hint of irregularity, the older *bugyo* Sakakibara Hida-no-kami initiated the process much as he had the former interrogation.

"What is your name and your profession?"

"My name is Father Antonio Gonzalez," the cleric said, keeping a steady gaze at Ferreira on his left. For Sawano Chuan, it seemed a rehashing of his own trial and he remained unperturbed. In truth he had been present at the trials of his fellow Jesuits and had never even deemed to speak to them.

"I am a religious of the Order of Saint Dominic," said Father Antonio, "and a superior of the three religious, who arrived ahead of us, and of the others of the order, who may eventually come in the future." At this Ferreira smiled with some modest amusement at the priest's audacity. The old Dominican had quite a fire in him.

"Did you have knowledge of the prohibition against the coming of religious to Japan?"

"Yes, I know the prohibition. But I have no other purpose in coming here than to preach the Good News of the Lord and his salvation, and to show the errors in which you and your people live." Father Antonio referred to no one in particular but the statement was meant to rouse them. It seemed to Ferreira an act of desperation or heroism. In circumstances like this, it was hard to tell the difference.

"Was the Governor of Manila aware of your departure? Did the Portuguese of Macao know about your coming? Are the Portuguese going to send you any financial help?" The rising volume of his voice and rapidity of the *bugyo's* questioning in concert with the oblique reference to Sawano Chuan iced the proceedings further.

"No sirs," Father Antonio replied, this time looking straight at the *bugyos*. "The Governor of Manila knew nothing, and the Portuguese even less." This seemingly ended the priest's unspoken exchange with Ferreira, and centered the attention on his own miserable circumstances.

"Your companions have told us that you bring some letters from Manila. Is it true?"

Father Antonio made his straightforward reply only to the older *bugyo*. "Yes, I bring four copies of a letter I wrote in Latin, for you and for a renegade priest who resides in Nagasaki."

"I believe he is referring to me," Ferreira replied tersely, addressing himself to the older *bugyo*.

Father Antonio handed the letter to Jomei, who proffered it to Ferreira—Sawano Chuan. The letter made an appeal to the apostate Jesuit priest to recommit himself to the faith. The letter also requested his mediation with the Japanese magistrates, to inform them that the nature of the Dominican's mission was purely religious instruction and not at all political in nature.

The letter in Latin was distributed to the two *bugyos* by one of the Japanese interpreters. The other interpreter was summoned by the younger *bugyo* to simultaneously translate its contents. Lorenzo watched intently, and wondered if this was what Father Antonio had hoped might occur. Gauging a slim opportunity to address his fellow Christians, the Dominican began to deliver a sermon about "our holy faith."

"No one who believes in him will be put to shame," he began, addressing the apostate clerics in Latin, citing part of Saint Paul's letter to the Romans. "The same Lord is Lord of all and is generous to all who call on him. But how are they to call on one in whom they have not believed? And how are they to believe in one of whom they have never heard? And how are they to hear without someone to proclaim him? And how are they to proclaim him unless they are sent? As it is written, 'How beautiful are the feet of those who bring good news!'"[3]

He was well into the third and fourth statement of his sermon when the two *bugyos* raised their fans in indignation. Realizing that the friar's Latin oration was not the same as the contents of his letters, they ordered Father Antonio gagged. The fact that the apostate priests said nothing to contradict the now quiet Dominican inflamed the *bugyos* enough that they turned their attention elsewhere. The younger *bugyo* Baba Saburozayemon motioned Lazaro of Kyoto to the fore, but a guard halted him a distance away because of his leprous condition. Lazaro, for his part, took additional steps backward in safety.

"Do the missionaries in Manila send letters and financial aid to the Christians in Japan?"

"I have been in Manila for some years, and every year ships left Manila for Macao," Lazaro answered, rattled. "It is possible that some help came from missionaries of Manila for those in Japan, via Macao galleons," he said, a bit generous with his own speculations.

This deduction gave enough weight to the *bugyos'* suspicions so that the magistrates ordered Lazaro of Kyoto to be further interrogated in a separate chamber. But their annoyance at Father Antonio had not subsided, and they commanded that he undergo the water torture. The apostate priests, including Ferreira, were dismissed. They bowed before the magistrates before leaving the chamber, but only Ferreira showed a similar courtesy toward Father Antonio. As he watched the letter delivered to Ferreira transfer to the hands of the *bugyos*, Lorenzo suspected that they had all been abandoned. Their only choice now was to do what Christ had done from his cross and commend themselves to the will of God.

# CHAPTER 16

While the guards led Father Antonio to the torture chamber, Lorenzo—now under Jomei's guard—followed apprehensively.

Father Antonio had a combined demeanor of resignation and defiance. They stripped him of his garments, and made him sit, while they forced gallons of water down his throat and into his stomach. Several times he vomited. Nearby, Lazaro of Kyoto heard Father Antonio's struggle and protests. Deeply agitated at what he heard, his speech faltered.

When Father Antonio could take in no more fluid, his tormentors wrestled him onto the ground and threw wooden planks over him. All at once three samurais jumped on the planks until the pressure they exerted forced a stream of runny waste and blood out of their victim. Below the planks the old priest coughed and wailed.

Lorenzo Ruiz watched in revulsion as this occurred about nine feet away from where he stood, immobilized by fright and speechless; it was as if Lorenzo's senses had been slammed out of him. Suddenly, at the center of his being, Lorenzo realized that this is what the other priests had suffered. He made an attempt to move, or even just round out his lips in verbal protest. But only words of prayer came to him. *Hail Mary, full of grace . . .* He could feel the sight of it all burning into his memory even as he watched it transpire before him. His eyelids flickered as if a light were about to extinguish. *Holy Mary, Mother of God . . .*

The *bugyos* ordered the friar to be taken into another chamber for what they called the *fumie,* the desecration of religious images that the Japanese had devised for Christians to affirm their decision to renounce their faith in Christ.

"Trample them," came the order. Images of the Blessed Virgin Mary, Saint Dominic, and other saints were positioned on the floor, affixed to a wooden board. Father Antonio did not respond. It was unclear to Lorenzo whether that was by choice, or simply from the trauma of the torture he had just experienced.

"Trample them!" the guard repeated, louder than before.

"You need not stamp on them, Father," Jomei said. "Just a light touch of your foot will do."

Father Antonio shook his head in defiance. The pride Lorenzo felt welling up in his heart was no less tangible than the tears that filled his eyes.

Then Jomei came forward and stamped on all the images one by one.

Father Antonio, overcome by the brutishness of his tormentors, ran toward the images and covered them with his body to prevent any further sacrilege. Though they were only representations of real people, they were sacred icons of those he loved, those who had gone before him in the faith. It was as if they had asked him to commit an abomination against his father and mother, his brothers and sisters. He could not do so, especially because earlier when the samurais were torturing him, these holy ones had come to his mind and provided him with the strength to carry on. Father Antonio knew that if he trampled on them, he would have crushed his own resolve. He raised his head and kissed the images of the saints and the Holy Mother of God, whose features—much as his own—had been damaged by repeated abuse.

Encouraged by the fidelity he witnessed, Lorenzo braced himself for whatever was about to be loosed upon him. *They mock us and what we cherish. Help me endure it to the end, Blessed Mother; by your prayers keep the devils of anger, discouragement, and fear from weakening my resolve,* he prayed.

The *bugyos* were incensed by what Father Antonio had done. The younger one, Baba Saburozayemon went over and slapped the old friar across the face. "You have seen these men trample on those images with their feet. You, too, will be trampled," he warned. "Severe punishment will fall on you and your companions, because you have dared to come to this country."

"You speak like the Pharisees," Father Antonio said, more keenly aware that the magistrates before him seemed to have more than just a cursory knowledge of the Christian faith. They had used the word "sin" instead of "crime." And this made their viciousness especially distasteful to him. These men knew, more than Jomei and the rest, what vile things they had committed. "I did not come for this," said the friar, trying and failing to raise himself up by an arm. "I came only to preach the way of salvation and lead these people to the knowledge of God."

Lazaro of Kyoto looked miserably into Father Antonio's eyes when he, too, was then brought into the water torture chamber. A gasp of revulsion arose in the room after the leper had been stripped naked. The sight of his disfigured body made Lorenzo wonder whether the man had not already suffered enough in his lifetime. *Should he be further subjected to torture, my Lord?*

After the first round of torment, Lazaro of Kyoto, through his gnarled expression, begged for mercy and began to falter in his faith. Father Antonio, who urged the poor leper on, was himself restrapped to the torture chair.

In the meantime, Jomei tried to deceive the old friar with taunts. He ranted about how the three Dominican clerics had abandoned their faith.

"Renounce! Renounce just like the others did," he yelled brassily as if he were beating down the Dominican with a gong.

But Father Antonio could not be dissuaded. He knew that his fellow Dominicans were true disciples, and had given themselves fully to their Lord and the mission the Lord sent them on. With great inner strength, Father Antonio would not allow doubt to lessen the trust he had in his brother priests. His courage edified the leper to the point that Lazaro of Kyoto withstood further pressures to abjure.

Lorenzo, observing the scene as if he were a spirit hovering above his own body, fidgeted in a corner of the room. *What of his wife and his three children? Would they ever even know what had happened to him?* The idea of not ever returning to the Philippines or breathing into the next day overwhelmed him with sadness. *Lord, strengthen me!* As the torture continued, Lorenzo beckoned one of the Japanese translators to his side.

"What is your name?" he asked, which baffled the interpreter. But Lorenzo thought only of befriending him in the moment.

"What's it to you?" At first the translator refused to divulge any information. His European name might elicit a wrong impression from the captive. But after a flash of insight, the translator replied, "My fellow scribe over there, his name is Pedro Rodriguez."

Lorenzo was at least right in his assumption and nodded. *At least one of them is an apostate Christian. Somehow, that thought brought him comfort.*

Seeing the relief in Lorenzo's face, he continued. "I? Antonio Carvalho."

This boosted Lorenzo's hopes and he asked the interpreter to come closer. "I want to tell you something in secret, sir Carvalho," he whispered.

"What do you want to say?"

At this, the older *bugyo* shifted his eyes toward the slightly built Filipino. He was not a priest. Nor did he appear to have any real significance in the group.

"I would like to know if . . ." the words came out grudgingly, but they were dislodged with a gulp of humiliation from his throat. "By renouncing my faith," he stammered, "will they spare me my life?" Lorenzo asked. Fear had tempted him to ask what was otherwise unthinkable.

"I cannot answer that question," said Carvalho, somewhat pleased. "You should ask it before the president of the tribunal," referring to the older *bugyo*.

The magistrate summoned the interpreter and they discussed the situation. "He is right, poor little man," said Sakakibara. Considering the usefulness of a Filipino scribe in his court, he thought about how it would demoralize the Dominican priests to have their protégé recant. However, the *bugyo* remained vague about the fate of Lorenzo Ruiz. He was not the kind of man to make promises.

Carvalho returned to the torture chamber. The expression on Father Antonio's face had transformed into one of inscrutable torment.

Lorenzo motioned again to the interpreter and begged for his indulgence.

"Sir, what I said to you earlier, I said it like an ignorant man, without knowing what I was saying. I am a Christian. And this I will profess until the hour of my death." The swift turnaround surprised Carvalho. "I shall give my life for God, if that is what he wants," Lorenzo continued. "Although I did not come to Japan to be a martyr, however . . . as a Christian, I shall give my life. And so, do with me as you please." By the time he had spoken the last word the interpreter had all but fled his side and reported Lorenzo's change of heart to the *bugyo*.

At this juncture Sakakibara ordered the torture of Lorenzo Ruiz. It was Jomei who carried out that order. But even after several attempts to break him, Lorenzo did not give in.

# CHAPTER 17

By the end of the day, Father Antonio, Lazaro of Kyoto, and Lorenzo Ruiz were conducted to their jail cells. There they found the other three captives awaiting them with a sincere, if weak, welcome. None of them expected that Father Antonio could last a week. At his age, internal hemorrhaging from the ordeal had already begun to sap the life from him, and a high fever had begun to take hold. Nonetheless, the joy they had at this reunion was not diminished.

"My sons, how good it is to be with you again," Father Antonio panted between deep yet painful gasps of breath.

Despite the pain and humiliation each of them had suffered, they managed to laugh weakly. And regardless of the labor it took them to breathe, they sang together verses of Psalm 133.

> How very good and pleasant it is when kindred live
> together in unity!
> It is like the precious oil on the head, running down
> upon the beard,
> on the beard of Aaron, running down over the collar
> of his robes.

It is like the dew of Hermon, which falls on the
mountains of Zion.
For there the Lord ordained his blessing, life
forevermore.

Their chanting alarmed the guards and they alerted Jomei immediately. He commanded his men to barge into the cell without delay and separate the men. Isolation was not half as bad for the rest as it seemed to be for Lazaro of Kyoto. Because he had wavered in his faith during the torture, guilt was beginning to eat at him.

"Ahoy, ahoy, my friends," he called out, as if they were yet at sea.

"Lazaro?"

"Yes, Father Vicente, it is I."

"So good to hear you." They all laughed weakly, thinking how ridiculous it was to be separated when the walls were so thin that they could still hear one another without difficulty.

"What is it, Lazaro?" asked Father Miguel, who was the strongest among them.

"I was wondering if your stomachs ached." They stifled a loud laugh.

"Please Lazaro, you are killing me," replied Father Guillermo. "No more jokes until we heal."

"I am sorry, Padre."

"What is it, Lazaro?" asked Father Miguel, once more.

"I must ask you something," said Lazaro of Kyoto. "I have committed a grievous fault today . . . and I am sorry to all of you and to the Lord. Can you forgive me my sin and my weakness?"

A silence descended upon them at that moment, a

blanket of quiet punctuated by not quite silent sniffles. And they stayed this way until they had spent all their tears.

"I knew you would repent," assured Father Antonio, his baritone but a low whisper now. "And I absolve you in the name of the Father, and of the Son, and of the Holy Spirit."

Outside the cell, Jomei listened to the prayers of the Dominicans and their two companions and strangely hoped that they might raise their voices again in chant. It had been a tiresome day. Even he was in need of some respite. But the men stayed quiet. Lorenzo counted Hail Marys on his fingers, reciting the Rosary until he succumbed to sleep. At the edge of consciousness he imagined that his family was praying the Rosary too, far away in Manila.

On September 23, Father Antonio and Lorenzo Ruiz were subjected to the torture of the needles as well. It was while they lay in their separate cells later that evening that the Filipino realized the height and breadth of their Christian commitment. For the first time in his life Lorenzo understood what love God had for him, and what suffering Jesus Christ had endured for the sake of that love. Lorenzo's heart filled with both joy and sorrow, as they offered their sacrifices at compline to the Divine Heart.

Though they could all hear one another, Father Antonio took it upon himself to speak to Lorenzo as if no one else were present but them. Lorenzo appreciated the kindness.

"My son, if you know something against us, tell them, and you will save your life." He had not overlooked Lorenzo's conversation with the Japanese interpreter, Carvalho, two days prior. But Father Antonio wanted to reassure Lorenzo that he loved him no less. They had each had moments of weakness.

"Father, I do not know anything against you," he said, regretting his own selfishness.

"What I do know is that these tormentors, by God's grace, cannot harm my soul. I do not want to be unfaithful, as they hope I will be. But I intend to cling to Christ, my life, my truth, and my way, even if it means clinging to him as he hangs on the cross."

On September 24 the *bugyos* commanded that the water torture again be administered to Father Antonio and Lorenzo Ruiz, because they were "stubborn and unyielding in their faith."

Lorenzo's stomach already ached from internal bleeding, so much so that severe pain made him double over. Father Antonio limped out from his cell and encouraged Lorenzo onward. They had arrived here in Nagasaki as mentor and protégé. But this day, made equal by the suffering they shared, they would be more like brothers.

In the chamber while they forced water yet again into the old friar, the older *bugyo* upbraided Lorenzo.

"Look at that priest. Did you see his feverishly bloody condition? What do you say of yourself, Filipino?"

"Me? What shall I say?" Lorenzo answered with impudence. "I don't know what to say. Why are you tormenting me? Kill me, and stop asking questions." Lorenzo's direct answer gave him the courage to be even bolder.

"I am a Filipino, son of a Chinese and a Filipina. I am married and have two sons and one daughter." The fury welled up inside him and he wept as he enunciated every word of his testimony. He made sure to repeat himself so that the Japanese interpreter Carvalho could take it down word for word.

"I could not stay in Manila because I had a quarrel with a Spaniard. I came with these Fathers in order to escape from Manila. They told me the galleon would stop in Formosa. But when we got there, I discovered that they, too, would hang me. So I decided to stay with the Fathers and come to Japan. I have spent a year imprisoned with them in Okinawa. Truthfully, when we reached Japan, I would have liked to return to Manila in the same sampan I left."

"Do you mean to say you want to recant?" asked the *bugyo*. "Look at your priest; look how he is suffering in all that blood."

"No, by no means, no. Do with me as you wish. I will never recant," affirmed Lorenzo, as the tormentors brought forth the sacred images for desecration.

The *bugyo* studied the man before him and persisted. "You are not a Spaniard. You are not even a priest. You are just an ordinary native of the Philippines. You made no vows, no covenant with anyone. You have nothing to lose, Filipino. But you have everything to gain: your life, your freedom and your family, even your job, if you only renounce this ridiculous faith."

"I am a Catholic and wholeheartedly accept death for God!"[1] Lorenzo cried out. "And if I had a thousand lives, I would offer them all to him." The strength he found within himself startled him and the others in the small chamber.

At this even the torturers ceased, and Father Antonio smiled in thanksgiving for Lorenzo's faith. His lips moved rapidly in praise and prayer.

Jomei took it upon himself to beat some sense into Lorenzo and he spared no mercy.

"Christians here are reduced to poverty because their property and all sources of livelihood are confiscated," Jomei screamed. "They are dispossessed of all their wealth. They have absolutely nothing."

"It is a miserable life to be a Christian here, I know," said Lorenzo. "You leave them nothing and yet, they have everything."

"But if you loved your family, you would renounce Christ, go on living, providing for them, protecting them." urged Jomei.

"Who am I to question God or his choice to die on the cross for us? He calls me to follow and says, 'If any want to become my followers, let them deny themselves and take up their cross and follow me.'[2] Why do you think he is lenient with the sinner but 'disciplines every son and daughter he receives?'"

"So you *want* to die?"

"No, I did not come here to be killed and be a martyr. If you think otherwise you are wrong. Even now, I beg the Lord to save me. But if by my death God is glorified and it is of benefit for others, I pray for strength."

"Are you saying that your death is of value?" Jomei asked derisively.

"No, not mine. I am nothing. Your salvation has already been won by the death of Christ."

"A simple act will win you your freedom. But you refuse; you are an idiot." Jomei's anger seemed somehow personal.

"To the world, what I am doing appears to be foolishness. But to the one who believes, it makes perfect sense. If God had given you the grace of faith and placed you here in my stead . . ."

"If our situations were reversed, you mean?" This tempered Jomei's ire somewhat.

"Yes. I would not expect your response to be any different than mine. This is what it means to believe: to give your whole heart and your life to the truth. Suffering is not the goal of a Christian, Master Jomei. But Christ has elevated suffering to sacrifice, and given it meaning. He bears salvation within himself like a mother bears a child, and gives us eternal life in Baptism through his cross and resurrection."

"Again, your cross. If I examined it a hundred times, I would not see the mystery in it. It is the image of a defeated man, punctured and tortured. There is no power in the cross, only suffering, humiliation, and death."

"You will think me insane for saying this, but I will say it anyway. When I look at the cross, and kiss it, it is because I believe. 'There lies life.' This is where the narrow path leads and none can enter heaven except by him. He is the key to our salvation. He opens the door to heaven. No one can see God in this life and live, which is perhaps why we are the ones who see him on the cross, so that even now, we can hope."

"And can he forgive me for what I do to you, his disciples?"

"Forgiveness and sacrifice together are the most powerful currency in the world. Jesus is the treasury of every real good and lasting joy. God already has forgiven us our sins. But have we learned to forgive one another? By grace, even now, I forgive you as God forgives me."

Jomei stopped briefly to collect his thoughts. But the doubts that Lorenzo had tried to plant in his mind enraged the samurai. Perhaps he was not just a simple Filipino after all. In frustration Jomei beat Lorenzo repeatedly until no further sound came from his mouth.

The Japanese translator Carvalho seemed almost absent in these proceedings. Yet, he had taken it upon himself to write exactly and in detail the words of this Filipino. As he did so, Carvalho suspected that he had recorded the testimony of a holy man.

In the evening, before Jomei enclosed the captives once again in their cells, Father Antonio begged for some wine to ease his agony and suffering. Deeply troubled, Jomei granted the friar's request.

The full moon had waxed the night before on the 23rd. This evening as the friars prayed compline, the last prayers of the night, the old Dominican's voice was absent. By morning it was discovered that Father Antonio had passed calmly in his sleep. His body was taken out in the morning, carried to Nishizaka Hill and cremated. Afterward his ashes were thrown out to sea. As had become the practice of Japan's secret Christians, they made their way up the hill and collected what was left of the remains, safeguarding them as holy relics. Within their prison the Dominicans offered prayers for their superior. His courage had won him quick release from his miseries, and the long-awaited welcome into just repose. He had lived in charity even toward his foes, and fortitude against the vileness of death.

Taking full advantage of Father Antonio's absence, the *bugyos* ordered that the prisoners be tortured three days more, this time in stepped-up haste to perform the *fumie*. The Japanese court surmised that the pressure to deny their faith would have been great before the sacred images, especially after the death of their Dominican superior. But it seemed that nothing could demoralize the prisoners. Instead, the death of Father Antonio seemed to urge them on. Some had come very close to dying. But having failed to dissuade them, the Japanese court ruled that their final sentence be handed down, and justice meted out by Jomei, the samurai executioner.

# CHAPTER 18

A light rain was falling that Wednesday morning, September 27. The pageantry of a public execution usually began early in the day and intensified by midmorning, when the greatest numbers of people were out and about in the streets. The official announcements had been posted throughout the city since Sunday, the day Father Antonio had died.

The announcement read: "Shogun Iemitsu, through his governors Sakakibara Hida and Baba Saburozayemon, has ordered the execution of these insane men, who dared to preach a foreign principle that is against the law of the land. These men are therefore scoundrels and criminals and should be exterminated without mercy." A caveat followed: "Let this execution be a warning to all others who will follow them and believe in their principles."

When Jomei arrived to release them from their cells, it was clear to Lorenzo that beneath the samurai's calm exterior was a discomfort approaching grief. A strange impulse to reach out to him stirred in Lorenzo's heart. "Faith and life are inseparable for me," Lorenzo said quietly to Jomei. "Life without faith would have been a life without any value. You are taking nothing from me."

One of the executioners shaved half Father Guillermo's scalp and painted it a scarlet red, exposing him to further mockery. "How sweet are your words to my taste, sweeter than honey to my mouth, O Lord,"[1] the friar prayed, as the two remaining priests were also shaved and painted.

Jomei, a bit weary, responded. "There is no sweetness, greatness, or victory for those who die on that hill."

Each of the Dominicans was hoisted on an unsaddled horse, propped up by humiliating signs naming their crimes. A forward contingent of about five men, two on horseback, three on foot, heralded their approach. The people who approached the prisoners as they made their way offered a study in contrasts. While some expressed disgust and hatred, others showed sorrow. One Spaniard who was present later described the scene.

"The five heroes marched on horseback in this order: First, the Japanese from Kyoto, that is Lazaro the Leper, who led his companions to the place of martyrdom. In the second place, there was the 'mestizo' Lorenzo Ruiz, giving honor to his country and to his pueblo of Binondo for having valiantly suffered for the Lord and for going joyfully to die for his Faith. The third was Father Vicente Shiwozuka de la Cruz, the Japanese, bravely confessing the Lord for whom he was suffering. The fourth place was Father Guillermo Courtet, so weak and feeble that he could hardly stay on the horse but strong enough to ride with his eyes raised to heaven, and the fifth and last was Father Miguel de Aozaraza, with a joyful and happy face, admired by those who were looking at him."[2]

Jomei and the other samurai guards took up the rear. The procession wound through the city streets—arriving under a heavy downpour at Nishizaka Hill. The five men were pulled off their mounts. Determined to carry out every detail of their execution, Jomei closely supervised the other samurais. They bound the men's legs and one arm tightly with ropes and rags. Then, pulling out their knives, the samurais cut two gashes in each of the prisoners' foreheads. Lorenzo shuddered with horror, and shook uncontrollably.

None of them could have begun to imagine what would happen next. Each man was moved, with difficulty, to the edge of a rancid pit filled with excrement and other waste. There, wooden planks were fitted around their waists. As the men were lowered upside down into the pit, the planks came to rest at the ground's surface. Suspended, the prisoners hung, weeping. Their eyes were barely clear enough to see that just below their slowly bleeding heads were sharpened spikes.

One arm, however, remained free to signal to the executioner a newfound willingness to apostatize and deny the faith. It was said that the device elicited such panic from Christians who had witnessed the torture that many rejected Christ simply by being brought in front of the pit.

Devised in 1633 by a Nagasaki *bugyo*, it was no wonder that the *ana-tsurushi* became the most extreme and effective threat against Christians. A Protestant Dutch observer, who was a factory manager at Hirado, once described the fears of those who were threatened by hanging in the pit.

"The greatness of this torment surpasses all others, being beyond all human strength to suffer and undergo except by those who are extraordinarily strengthened from above. This extreme [measure] has indeed by reason of its [continued use] forced many to renounce their religion, and some of them, who hanged for two or three days, assured me that the pains they had endured were wholly insufferable, no fire, no torture equaling their languor and violence."[3]

Even for a seasoned executioner, the process was almost unbearable to witness. The agony of dying in the *ana-tsurushi* was both extreme and prolonged. Walking as far from the men as he could, Jomei realized how grateful he was that only the lower half of his victims' bodies was visible to him. He wondered if he would be able to obey his orders had that not been the case.

As they wasted there in the pits, blood dripping through the gashes in their temples to the rhythm of their heartbeats, the Dominican company could count the seconds of their agony. The throbbing accompanied them into the night. In the passage of this slow drip into oblivion, time somehow became suspended in an extraordinary moment of darkness—abandonment. Each one of them felt the total absence of the God who they believed loved them and for whom they had given up their lives. Yet, in faith they knew God was there.

It was perhaps in the twelfth hour of their agony that Father Guillermo began to stir.

"My God, my God, why have you forsaken me?" he cried, loud enough to snap Jomei and the other samurai to attention.

"O my God, I cry by day, but you do not answer; and by night, but find no rest."

Other fragments of Psalm 22 flooded Lorenzo's mind.

> In you our ancestors trusted;
> they trusted, and you delivered them.
> To you they cried, and were saved;
> in you they trusted, and were not put to shame.
> But I am a worm, and not human;
> scorned by others, and despised
> by the people . . .
> But you, O Lord, do not be far away off! . . .
> Deliver my soul from the sword . . .

The *bugyos* held out the hope that condemned Christians under these excruciating circumstances would still renounce their faith in public. To this end, they offered the Dominicans a final opportunity to apostatize. Jomei ordered that the pits be opened and the accused be given a ration of food.

In a surprising tone bordering on supplication, Jomei spoke to the condemned, "Here, take something to eat,"[4] begged Jomei. "Please, it is for your good as well as ours."

"We want nothing," said Father Vicente.

"We ask pardon for the trouble you have taken on account of us," replied Father Miguel.

In frustration, Jomei ordered the wooden planks be readied once more. But before closing in on Lorenzo he made a hushed confession. "You know, I called you an idiot. And you are," Jomei began in halting Spanish.

"What of it?" Lorenzo gasped. "Nothing will change that now. But despite all that you have done, I forgive you. God forgives you, and I forgive you."

"You do not understand. Your life means nothing to me. But think of what it means to your family, your wife and children. The priests can die for their God. They have committed themselves to that in their vows. But your vow is to your wife and family. Even a Christian knows that. Listen, Filipino, what does it matter to me? My wife was once a Christian, but three years ago she, too, hung here on this hill, one of the first to undergo the *ana-tsurushi*. And my master, an apostatized *daimyo*, tested my resolve and loyalty to his service. Think what it was like to supervise the execution of my own wife. Think! She abjured for the sake of our infant son. Think of that every second you are in the pit. For the sake of your family, I beg you, Lorenzo, renounce your faith."

Lorenzo was quiet until he began to cough while taking labored breaths. He looked intently into Jomei's face. "My wife, too, is a Christian. She knows that all who enter heaven come by the narrow gate," Lorenzo replied softly, "purged of all that is undesirable to the Lord. From this pit I will cry to the Lord. God will hear me. He will take care of my family. He will preserve them on my account."

Incredulous, Jomei lowered Lorenzo and the others into the pit once more and sealed it saying, "You do not have a thousand lives, Lorenzo—only one. But now you shall have a thousand deaths to offer to your God. Do you think he will be satisfied?"

In the darkness of the pit, death approached slowly. Lorenzo flowed in and out of consciousness almost as if he was dreaming. But though he was bound, his mind wandered freely. The house he grew up in, his father teaching him how to write Chinese characters, the spicy scent of his mother's cooking: these came to him as more than memories. Then Rosario, their two boys, and the little girl who lit up when he came home at the end of the day appeared at last. They were smiling. Lorenzo prayed for all who had helped him: for Guapo and the ship's captain and cook, the Chinese fishermen, and the Japanese courtesan in Okinawa—what was her name?—and lastly for the prisoners and guards that had filled the air with chant when they left. And in this prayer he found peace.

By the third day the *bugyos* ordered that the prisoners be beheaded. The magistrates were preparing to go off on a hunt and wanted the execution completed before they left the city.

When Jomei raised the prisoners from the pit, he discovered that both Lorenzo Ruiz and Lazaro of Kyoto were already dead. He took the three priests—Father Guillermo Courtet, Father Miguel de Aozaraza, and Father Vicente Shiwozuka de la Cruz and delivered the final stroke with his sword. But before Father Miguel was killed he quoted Saint Antoninus, a Dominican saint, "To serve God is to reign."

Some who were there at the end said that they saw the tough executioner crying. After the corpses of the condemned were thrown onto a fire, their ashes were thrown into the sea. Jomei and his fellow samurai broke camp and left the hill in silence.

~~~

Three months later, through a covert network of communication by underground Christians, word of the martyrs' deaths finally reached the monastery in the old Santo Domingo Church along the Pasig River in Manila. It was Christmas.

"Rosario?" The new Dominican superior knocked on the door of the little house in Binondo. "Rosario, I have news."

"What is it, Father—is it from Lorenzo?" she asked with growing excitement.

"No, but it is about Lorenzo. Where are the children? You must sit down."

The priest told her all that had been relayed to him as gently as he could. Her tears flowed in disbelief.

"A martyr? In Japan?"

"Yes, Rosario, your husband is a saint. He gave his life for the faith. No one can do more."

"If my husband is a saint, Father, then he will still take care of us. God will not forget."

"No one will forget Lorenzo. No one."

All the churches in Manila tolled their bells for hours to honor the generous sacrifice the six men had made. The Governor, Sebastian Hurtado de Corcuera, paid his respects to the Dominican provincial superior. And in Masses that the

Dominicans held for their glorious brethren, the image of the Mother of God was decorated with garlands of white jasmine flowers and small yellow roses.

Ultimately news of what had happened reached the pontiff in Rome, Pope Urban VIII. While there was nothing new about martyred religious, many were intrigued to hear that two others had poured out their lives alongside the Dominican priests: a leper, and a native Filipino layman with a wife and three children.

It was that thought that dogged Jomei in the years that followed. How could a man like Lorenzo, one with a wife and family, choose his faith over his life? In the weeks of torture he endured and the three days of excruciating pain and fear, Jomei surmised that Lorenzo must have made that choice at least a thousand times. What he did not know, or yet understand, was why.

# EPILOGUE

"*Get some water. Hurry, my child.*"
The urgency in Jomei's voice frightened her. Aiko had never seen her grandfather in this state of agitation before. Running to fill a pitcher, she almost stumbled. "Pour the water on my head," Jomei instructed. Aiko hesitated for a mere breath of a moment, then began to tilt the jug. "Say these words," Jomei continued, "'I baptize you, in the name of the Father, and of the Son, and of the Holy Spirit.'" Knowing this was not a time for questions, the girl did as she was told. Then, as if some vast weight had been lifted off him, Jomei laid himself out on the bamboo mat with her assistance, crossed his hands over his chest, and closed his eyes. His face glowed with peace.

Aiko was mystified. Kneeling beside her grandfather, it seemed that an atmosphere of finality hovered around him. His shrunken form had never looked so small to her as it did at this moment on the floor. She gazed at the hand that had penned bold calligraphy on scrolls of handmade paper, all tucked for safekeeping within the rafters of their house. Aiko touched his head where the water was still dripping, then put her hand to her own head. A flood of emotion filled her.

152

Rushing to the door, Aiko saw her parents coming from the fields. She ran toward them waving her hands frantically. Aiko's father froze. A circle of leaves blew around him as he watched his wife Toshi run up the steps.

Toshi burst into the room without removing her shoes. Stooping down, she placed an ear against Jomei's chest to listen to the old man's heart. Aiko held her breath as her mother closed her eyes so as to be able to hear even the faintest of beats. Silence. Jomei was dead.

Aiko looked one way and then another—at her grandfather lying on the floor, with her mother beside him, and then along the path to her approaching father. Ichito seemed to sink into the ground with each step.

Toshi took the water pitcher from Aiko's hands and wet the old man's lips as was the custom. *Did the guest leave sooner than expected?* Aiko wondered to herself. *Did he take my ojiisan with him?* Not knowing what else to do, Aiko gathered the two teacups, one still full. She knew she was not supposed to weep when bad things happened, but Aiko opened her mouth and cried.

〜〜

A few days after Jomei's passing, Aiko opened one of his scrolls and began to read. It felt as if her *ojiisan* was there, speaking with her again.

"*Though the way Lorenzo Ruiz died changed my mind about the man,*" Jomei had written, "*the thought that I had taken away the life of such a dignified man seized me with enormous guilt and shame. I wanted to purge myself of this memory, to save face for my family and me. For a samurai, it was as natural as one's duty.*

"*As a matter of experience, I learned that you cannot live a year with your enemies and not absorb the hate they* have for you. But what of the man whose enemies love him, as a brother and as a friend? I cannot say I believe it still. But one's life is forever changed by a captive who extends to his foe the true hand of mercy. Ought it not have been the other way around? Shouldn't it have been the captive begging for mercy, groveling for compassion?

"In the death of Lorenzo Ruiz, I was much like the Roman centurion who was charged with killing the Christ. After all was said and done, he managed to offer this bit of truth: 'Truly this man was the Son of God. This man was innocent.'

"I will not tire you with the tale of how a prisoner and one condemned to die became my teacher long after his death. Such twists of fate present such an over-dramatized tale of conversion. But I will tell you that Lorenzo Ruiz visited me in a dream many years after we had thrown his ashes into the sea. He said that at my death, he would be there with his Lord. At first I feared this prophecy. Would he taunt me at the moment when I was weakest and most unable to defend myself?

"But every autumn, at the anniversary of his execution, I began to believe that this meeting was something not to be feared but welcomed. So in keeping with the promise, I prepared myself for it, as would any samurai who had been chosen by his daimyo to be in the service of the emperor. But it was as if no one on earth was worthy enough or able to lead me to this God and yet there I was, hoping. And that is what you witnessed at the first winds of autumn.

"Perhaps what angered me most about Ruiz was that he left his family behind after a false accusation of murder was made against him. How was he going to prove his innocence, so far away from his country? Didn't his reputation matter to him at all? What does a man have, after all, but his name held in honor and respect? If he gives that up, what else is left? I learned that the humble man has more to spare than his reputation. He lays down his will and his life, everything—except he does not yield his hope in God. Unbound by anything a respectable man holds dear, the humble man is free.

"There was something about how Lorenzo, who even when stripped of everything, retained his dignity. And this I could respect even as I supervised his execution on Nishizaka Hill. I took nothing away that he did not already freely give. Lorenzo saw something more after death that was his and I could not take it away from him. What was it? They gave up their lives for something more, a meaning I also wanted.

"As it is written in Scripture: 'The kingdom of heaven is like treasure hidden in a field, which someone found and hid; then in his joy he goes and sells all that he has and buys that field. Again, the kingdom of heaven is like a merchant in search of fine pearls; on finding one pearl of great value, he went and sold all that he had and bought it.' —Matthew 13:44–46.

"So believing I had committed a grave injustice, I asked to be released from my daimyo's service. After much deliberation, his lordship agreed on the condition that I keep the reason for this departure a secret. The example of those I had put to death led me to acknowledge that faith in Christ was not for the weak. But it was the appearance of Lorenzo Ruiz in a dream that brought me to embrace that faith myself.

"Though I didn't know exactly how, I wanted to serve. The hidden Christians found it difficult to trust me because of my role in executing their martyrs. So, I decided to help those who were further removed from the community—the lesser Christians, those who turned away from their faith *under duress, but regretted their cowardice and reverted to their faith. I turned my efforts to farming—to feed my family and those on the fringe. And I took up calligraphy once again. After I had forsaken all else and even offered my wife her freedom to leave me with our son—thankfully she had stayed. I knew not why. But was not Lorenzo Ruiz himself a recorder, an* escríbano, *like one of the priests had mentioned? I knew then what was to be my duty: to write down all that I had seen."*

Aiko knew immediately what she had to do. Quietly, she wrapped the scrolls in a blanket and made plans to take them to the house of a family thought to be secret Christians.

When she got there, a small and unassuming older man answered the door.

"Look," Aiko said, bowing quickly. "Perhaps you will not believe me, but I have read them. These are scrolls that attest to the lives of Catholic martyrs. Can I leave them with you for safekeeping?" Aiko gently unwrapped them, and offered them to the man. Astonished, he took them from her. "They were written by my grandfather. He is gone now, but he was there when they died. His words tell how under his command such an execution took place."

"Why do you come to me with these writings?" asked the man, wondering if this was some kind of trap.

"Grandfather asked me to baptize him with running water," she said.

"And what did you do?" asked the secret Christian.

"I prayed the words."

"And what do you want from us?"

"The same for myself," she said.

# PRAYER TO SAN LORENZO RUIZ FOR THE SICK

Beloved Lorenzo de Manila and Martyr Companions (San Antonio Gonzalez, San Guillermo Courtet, San Miguel de Aozaraza, San Vicente Shiwozuka de la Cruz and San Lazaro of Kyoto)—to you do we come for help. Help us to have the same faith and love that you had for God. We call upon you today on behalf of our ailing beloved ones.

By your prayers and intercession obtain for them not only comfort and peace for their souls, but also vigor, strength, and health for their bodies. We place our entire confidence in you because we know that God loves you and that you care for us. We earnestly pray that our sick ones be purified and revitalized in every cell, tissue, nerve and organ, so that the bodily limbs may function effectively again. Through your powerful intercession help our sick to receive the grace of God's miraculous compassion, so that they will be completely whole again, and thereby be able to continue serving God in this life to the best of their strength and to attain the salvation to which you arrived. Amen.

Prayer from the Chapel of San Lorenzo Ruiz,
378 Broome Street, New York, New York 10013.
Permission granted by Father Erno Diaz,
Director of the San Lorenzo Ruiz Chapel in New York City.

# Notes

## Prologue

1. Ritual suicide by cutting the abdomen. It was practiced by high-ranking Japanese of the military class in lieu of execution or to avoid disgrace. Also called hara-kiri.

2. A feudal lord who administered vast estates and served at the pleasure of the shogun.

3. Both *sofu-san* and *ojiisan* mean "grandfather." The former is used when directly addressing a grandfather. The latter is used when one wishes to use the noun "grandfather."

## Chapter 1

1. The carabao is a type of water buffalo.

2. New Spain was land in the Western Hemisphere owned and governed by Spain during the period from 1535–1821. In the Americas this land comprised Florida in the east and everything north of present-day Panama to California in the west.

3. A large three-masted ship with two or more decks. It served as either a merchant ship, as in this case, or a warship.

## Chapter 2

1. A person employed in the loading and unloading of ships.

2. Galleons had fore-castles and after-castles—from the after-castle handheld firearms were discharged to protect the ship.

# CHAPTER 3

1. An enclosed superstructure above the main deck at the stern of the ship.

# CHAPTER 4

1. See Pablo E. Pérez-Mallaína, *Spain's Men of the Sea: Daily Life on the Indies Fleets in the Sixteenth Century,* trans. Carla Rahn Phillips (Baltimore: The Johns Hopkins University Press, 1998),141.

# CHAPTER 5

1. See Pérez-Mallaína, *Spain's Men of the Sea.*

# CHAPTER 6

1. Pérez-Mallaína, *Spain's Men of the Sea,* 177–179.

2. Job 9: 8–12

# CHAPTER 10

1. This refers to military rule by a shogun that was established by Tokugawa Ieyasu in 1600 and lasted over 250 years until 1868.

# CHAPTER 12

1. 1 Cor 1:18

# CHAPTER 13

1. See Jose Maria S. Luengo, *Lorenzo Ruiz: The Filipino Protomartyr in Nagasaki* (Indianapolis: Philippine Heritage Endowment Publications, 1984), 108.

2. Lk 19:42–44

3. The Spanish *pan de oro* refers to gold leaf.

4. There is no specific information on the currency referred to as a "manila."

5. *Barra de oro,* a 22-carat gold ingot, also was a unit of currency in imperial Spain and its colonies.

6. Fidel Villaroel, *Lorenzo Ruiz, the Protomartyr of the Philippines and His Companions* (Manila: Daughters of Saint Paul, 1979), 88.

# Chapter 14

1. Mt 26:39

2. Ps 22:14

3. See Antonio y Pedro Rodriguez Carvallo, *The Memoirs of the Interpreters of Nagasaki,* apud El Catálogo de Father Diego Rodriguez (Manila, 1650).

# Chapter 15

1. Mk 8:34–37

2. Literally translates as "pit and pendant." In this torture device the condemned were made to hang upside down from a horizontal beam set at about six feet above ground, attached on its ends to vertical posts affixed to the ground. Because the condemned could be swung, it was referred to as a pendant.

3. Rom 10:11-12, 14

# Chapter 17

1. See Celso Carunungan, *To Die a Thousand Deaths: A Novel on the Life and Times of Lorenzo Ruiz* (Manila: Social Studies Publications, 1980).

2. Mt 16:24

# Chapter 18

1. Ps 119:103

2. *81 L'Osservatore Romano* (English version). Special edition on the occasion of the beatification of Lorenzo Ruiz in Manila (March, 1981), 16; Villaroel, 270.

3. Villaroel, 120.

4. See Francis Caron, apud Villaroel, *Lorenzo Ruiz, Protomartyr,* 120; Protomartyr of the Philippines, "Boletin Eclesiastico de Filipinas, Missionary Projection" (Manila: University of Santo Tomas, 1965).

# Sources

## Books

Arcilla, Jose S., SJ. *The Spanish Conquest*. Hong Kong: Asia Publishing Company Limited, 1998.

Elliott, J.H. *Imperial Spain 1469–1716*. London, England: Penguin Books, 2002.

Guilmartin, John, Jr. *Galleons and Galleys*. London: Cassell & Co, 2002.

"Holy Bible: Revised Standard Version, Catholic edition," San Francisco: Ignatius Press, 1952.

Konstam, Angus. *Spanish Galleon 1530-1690*. Oxford, United Kingdom: Osprey Publishing, 2004.

Luengo, Jose Ma. S., PhD. *Lorenzo Ruiz: The Filipino Protomartyr in Nagasaki*. Indiana: Philippine Heritage Endowment Publications, 1984.

Pérez-Mallaína, Pablo E. Translated by Carla Rahn-Phillips. *Spain's Men of the Sea: Daily Life on the Indies Fleets in the Sixteenth Century*. Baltimore: The Johns Hopkins University Press, 1998.

Ratti, Oscar and Adele Westbrook. *Secrets of the Samurai: The Martial Arts of Feudal Japan*. New Jersey: Castle Books, 1999.

Rahn Phillips, Carla. *Six Galleons for the King of Spain: Imperial Defense in the Early Seventeenth Century*. Baltimore: The Johns Hopkins University Press, 1986.

Villaroel, Fidel, O.P. *Lorenzo Ruiz, the Protomartyr of the Philippines and His Companions*. Manila: Daughters of Saint Paul, 1979 [basis for court transcriptions as noted by Fr. Jose Ma. Luengo].

*L'Osservatore Romano*. Edicion Semanal en la lengua Española, el Primer Martir Filipino.

Vaticano, 1 de Marzo de 1981 [description of the needle torture as cited by Fidel Villaroel, O.P. and Fr. Jose Ma. Luengo].

Endo, Shusaku, *Silence*, trans. William Johnston. New York: Taplinger Publishing Company, 1980.

## Web Resources:

http://www.vatican.va/holy_father/john_paul_ii/speeches/1987/october/documents/hf_jp-ii_spe_19871018_comunita-filippina_en.html

http://www.newadvent.org/cathen/15218b.html

http://www.historyguide.org/earlymod/lecture6c.html

http://redalyc.uaemex.mx/redalyc/pdf/361/36100108.pdf

http://www.coins.nd.edu/ColCoin/ColCoinIntros/Sp-Gold.intro.html

http://www.chapelofsanlorenzoruiz.org/prayer.html

# About the Author

Susan Tan is a freelance writer of several magazine, newspaper, and Internet articles. She has a dual degree in behavioral sciences and communication arts from Assumption College in Makati City, Philippines, and a graduate degree in journalism from Medill School of Journalism, Northwestern University, Evanston, Illinois.

# *Catholic* Fiction

Pauline Teen promises you stories that:

- ☑ reflect your life experience
- ☑ deal with tough topics
- ☑ take your questions seriously
- ☑ have a sense of humor
- ☑ don't talk at you, over you, or down to you
- ☑ explore living your faith in the real world

At Pauline, we love a good story and aspire to continue the long tradition of Christian fiction.* Our books are great reads. But they are meant to engage your faith by accepting who you are here and now while inspiring you to recognize who God calls you to become.

*Think of classics like *The Hobbit, The Chronicles of Narnia, A Christmas Carol, Ben Hur,* and *The Man Who Was Thursday.*

**Who:** The Daughters of St. Paul

**What:** Pauline Teen—linking your life to Jesus Christ and his Church

**When:** 24/7

**Where:** All over the world and on www.pauline.org

**Why:** Because our life-long passion is to witness to God's amazing love for all people!

**How:** Inspiring lives of holiness through: APPS, digital media, concerts, websites, social media, videos, blogs, books, music albums, radio, media literacy, DVDs, ebooks, stores, conferences, bookfairs, parish exhibits, personal contact, illustration, vocation talks, photograph! writing, editing, graphi- marketin

**BOOKS & MEDIA**

The Daughters of St. Paul operate book and media centers at the following addresses. Visit, call, or write the one nearest you today, or find us at www.pauline.org.

CALIFORNIA
3908 Sepulveda Blvd, Culver City, CA 90230     310-397-8676
935 Brewster Avenue, Redwood City, CA 94063     650-369-4230
5945 Balboa Avenue, San Diego, CA 92111     858-565-9181

FLORIDA
145 SW 107th Avenue, Miami, FL 33174     305-559-6715

HAWAII
1143 Bishop Street, Honolulu, HI 96813     808-521-2731
Neighbor Islands call:     866-521-2731

ILLINOIS
172 North Michigan Avenue, Chicago, IL 60601     312-346-4228

LOUISIANA
4403 Veterans Memorial Blvd, Metairie, LA 70006   504-887-7631

MASSACHUSETTS
885 Providence Hwy, Dedham, MA 02026     781-326-5385

MISSOURI
9804 Watson Road, St. Louis, MO 63126     314-965-3512

NEW YORK
64 West 38th Street, New York, NY 10018     212-754-1110

PENNSYLVANIA
Philadelphia—relocating     215-676-9494

SOUTH CAROLINA
243 King Street, Charleston, SC 29401     843-577-0175

VIRGINIA
1025 King Street, Alexandria, VA 22314     703-549-3806

CANADA
3022 Dufferin Street, Toronto, ON M6B 3T5     416-781-9131